THE SINS OF MRS. EMA

THE SINS OF MRS. EMA

By

MIRELA KANINI

Your Author Journey Begins Here

Quantity Purchases:
Companies, professional groups, clubs, and other organizations may qualify for special terms when ordering quantities of this title.
For information, email info@ebooks2go.net,
or call (847) 598-1150 ext. 4141.
www.ebooks2go.net

Published in the United States by eBooks2go, Inc.
1827 Walden Office Square, Suite 260, Schaumburg, IL 60173

ISBN: 978-1-5457-5471-9

Library of Congress Cataloging in Publication

Contents

Chapter 1

Present time...

The airplane landed on time at the Tirana airport. The mesmerizing, uncountable lights of the city and high-rises of America were now replaced by the half-lit, half-asleep scene of my hometown. A young, curvy, black-haired woman with a loud voice was trying to wake up her four- or five-year-old son, who seemed to be enjoying a lengthy, deep sleep. She was speaking English to him.

"Honey, wake up. Grandma is waiting for you."

The little boy, who looked almost disturbed that his sleep—or perhaps his dream—was interrupted, was rubbing his eyes and looking around, trying to figure out what was happening. People in a hurry were pulling out their luggage, and it seemed, for a moment, that the long trip had shortened their patience. As for myself, I was trying to be calm and control my emotions and excitement—they felt like were going to explode at any moment—thinking that everyone could notice. But the fact was that no one was paying attention to me. It was simply in my subconscious; no one could tell that my heart was about to jump outside my body. I pulled my luggage down, almost tripping over it, and started dragging it through the tiny corridor of the airplane. I felt lightheaded and, for a moment, thought that I might have gotten sick from the ice-cold air that had been blowing from everywhere. Every passenger except me had kept the air conditioning on and I couldn't understand why they weren't bothered by it.

"Ema!"

"Toni, ah! I am finally here."

Suddenly I found myself lifted a little into the air and wrapped up in Toni's muscular arms.

"I love you," he whispered and kissed me directly on my lips. "How was your trip, love? Are you tired?"

"Not bad at all, superman," I teased him while instinctively touching his arms.

Toni smiled, showing his white teeth and making a cute, apologetic gesture, as if to say "It's not my fault that that I'm that handsome." We were standing in the middle of the crowd and hadn't taken our eyes off each other. It was like we couldn't get enough of exploring all the details of one another's features while everyone around us was in a hurry to get out of there.

"You are so beautiful, my love. Do you know that?"

"No. It's the first time I'm hearing it," I said, smiling at him. "So are you..." I continued with a lowered voice.

Toni put his hand around my shoulders and directed me toward the exit. At this moment nothing existed for me anymore. I couldn't see the people around me; nothing mattered because, as far as I was concerned, the world had only one person in it. His body odor, mixed with the scent of whatever shampoo or cologne he used, added to the warm temperature that I was feeling being welded to him, were all extremely attractive. It had given me a feeling like I was drunk without drinking, if that's how being drunk felt. I wouldn't know because I had never drank enough to get drunk in my life. Maybe it was more like I was high instead but I had never done any kind of drugs either. Somehow I now knew how it felt to be on those things. One thing I knew for sure was that I wanted this feeling to last, if not forever, for as long as possible. When we were finally in the parking lot, Toni kissed my hair and thanked me for coming. He was having a hard time believing I was there and I didn't know why.

"Pinch me so I can believe that you're here for real."

"Where do you want me to start?" I asked, pinching his chest.

"I still can't believe it," he said, now protecting himself from me because I was about to pinch him all over.

"How about now? Do you believe it now or will you have to wait until after I turn you black and blue from pinching?"

"Oh, my sweetheart. Now I do. You made me the happiest man alive today, Ema."

He gave me a long kiss before we finally made it into his car.

"I hope you're not disappointed by this face," he said, pointing toward himself. "Maybe it does not meet your expectations."

"You just read my mind. What on earth I was thinking, for God's sake? To make a trip from the other side of the world only to see a face like that? I must suffer the consequences now," I said, trying to keep a straight face.

"Ha ha ha! Oh God, if you only knew how much I love you, Ema."

We kissed again, from inside his car this time and for even longer.

"We have a long ride ahead and might hit some heavy traffic along the way. You can rest a little, or maybe take a nap if you want. That might be the only sleep you'll get while you're here the next few days," Toni said, looking over at me and giving me a wry smile.

"Are you planning to torture me or something? And would you tell me where we're going please?"

"Ah, I can't. It's a secret. Or to be more precise, it's a surprise."

"Why do I feel like a character in a sadistic horror movie?" I tried to look worried but couldn't keep the smile from my face.

"Ha, ha, I don't know, my love, but one thing is for sure—your imagination is wild."

3

"I have to agree with that. My tendency is to be skeptical and think about the dark side that people don't show, even while believing in their goodness and kindness."

"For instance, you might suspect that I am a serial killer and that I might take you somewhere far away, in a remote area, but using your seductive, charming ways, you convince me to leave you alive, right? And then I let you live day after day thanks to my change of heart."

"Yes, something like that, my sultan. How did you turn this into a story out of 'One Thousand and One Night?"

We started laughing, then we kissed and stayed with our lips welded together for a minute and our eyes on the road. I moved to my seat and, while lying there comfortably, I enjoyed the scenery of the villages we were leaving behind. Farms and land whose color had turned yellow and brown; lonely trees who had lost most of their leaves; unhappy cows who were chewing quietly on a few pieces of grass, which were hard to find that time of year. On the side of the road, you couldn't miss some farmers who looked cold and who were dressed so lightly in old and faded clothes. Their faces held deep wrinkles and their dry and damaged hands were the proof of their hard life. They spent all day every day on the side of those roads, getting covered with dust and sniffing the smoke of passing cars just to make a buck selling their goods. It was the chestnut season and suddenly I felt nostalgic for my childhood. I almost choked up in tears. Toni must have noticed because he asked me if I ever thought how my life would have been if I'd never left the country. I told him that I did think about that—quite often in fact—and, since he thought I had such a vivid imagination, I had truthfully built all those scenarios up in my mind about what I would have done with my life if I had never escaped to the far Western world.

"Do you think you would have done the same thing, professionally?"

"I think so. What I do for a living is something I passionately love doing. I feel that being a psychologist chose me more than I chose it. It suits me, and I don't know if I could do anything else better. Even though, in my early years, I wanted to be a journalist. Unfortunately, in this country I was never able to fulfill my dreams. I found everything I needed in my life in America. Maybe things have changed around here these days and it's better, but for me the memories of my homeland are bittersweet..."

It is said that things happen for a reason. I would never have guessed that one of the countries the company I worked for would choose to do business with was Albania. Since I left many years ago without returning, I was interestedly following the whole democratic progress of my country. It was obvious that it was a long, endless road with a lot being done and a lot more still to do. The company I worked for was supported by government programs and private sponsors to help abused women around the world. In some countries we would open centers with shelters for the ones who ran away from their abusers, boyfriends, or pimps. Through those programs, they would rehabilitate and earn the right to attend schools or courses in America. During that kind of mission, I met Toni. The company he was working for as an accountant and running all of their finances was one of the biggest sponsors of this country. Toni's background was as an engineer and, when I met him, he was on the road to getting promoted to a director of the company. During those two weeks of working next to him, I intensively felt something good. I didn't know what it was, but at least I felt understood. He was a true gentleman and would never say anything inappropriate or make comments and compliments like most of the other guys do on that side of the planet. Actually, I was under the impression that he was careful to hide some kind of shyness he felt while we were traveling in the company's van. He was trying to be polite and act naturally when we were stuck together like sardines inside the van, overly packed with people going to work. They didn't seem to keep their distance and stayed so close and smashed into me while Toni was trying to respect my space. One day he got the courage to ask me out for lunch and some historic sightseeing. We felt an instant connection and an immediate attraction despite the fact that we had just met. A certain magnetism was inevitable once you noticed a similar way of thinking or viewing life. We understood each other without even saying a word, only by looking into each other's eyes. When we talked, we would finish each other's sentences. I was drawn to him; his honesty, his sincerity, his opinions, and his sense of humor were making me fall for him uncontrollably. I would continue to laugh at his jokes even when I was alone at my place. We could talk about anything together without the need to be reserved or politically correct, and it felt good to be ourselves. One time he mentioned that he felt like he'd known me his whole life, and yet there wasn't enough time in this life to get to know me. He said that everything we were experiencing felt so familiar and I was either like someone he had known before or had always been with him somehow. I mentioned that we must have met in a different life. He smiled, admitting that this theory has crossed his mind too and he asked me to give him some idea of what eras we might have been together. I told him that I felt like we had lived in Chicago during World War II, and we were filthy rich, big manufacturers.

"No. I was a banker," interrupted Toni, acting so serious, like I was altering the true facts.

"You and your husband were factory owners because you were married when I met you. But later, you left everything behind. It's a very complicated story, let's leave it at that," he continued, with that sense of humor that allowed him to get away with pretty much anything. I got the hint and pretended that it was a joke.

He got very quiet for a few minutes after that and asked me if it would be possible for us to continue our friendship after I returned to America.

"I don't mean to be rude and inconsiderate, Ema, but it would mean a lot to me if we could stay in touch with each other. I must say that you are a very special woman and one of the most interesting people I know."

I wouldn't have been able to say no even if I wanted to. I was already hooked...

Chapter 2

I did take a nice nap while Toni was driving, and I'm not sure if I woke up from his sharp braking or from the cool air entering through the half-open window. For a moment it felt like I had slept for hours, only to find out that only thirty minutes had passed. I looked at Toni, who was driving quietly. It seemed like a permanent smile was stamped on his face, but that could have been my imagination. Here and there he would look at me with his green eyes that shone like two emeralds contoured with thick, dark lashes. He closed the window instinctively right after he thought I was shivering in my seat. He was always doing those little caring gestures that would melt my heart. Interestingly we had a number of these unspoken gestures flowing between us like we had lived together for years and knew what to expect. The same thing happened when we talked online. We would understand if something was bothering one another during the first sentence. It didn't matter that we were oceans away, on opposite sides of the world.

"Are you still cold, babe?"

"No, thank you."

"Is there any reason why you have that big smile on your face, my love?" said Toni.

"Nothing important. I just like your devotion, that's all." I said.

"Yeah, like a loyal dog, no doubt." Toni stuck his tongue out and made that dog face in such a cute way that made me laugh. Part of that laughter came from the comparison and the way people joked around here. Then he bit his lip from the inside. That particular gesture did something to me and he knew it. I think he did it purposely in a provocative way.

We seemed to be approaching the place where we would be spending the next few days together and Toni opened the window again.

"Do you smell anything, hon?"

"Yeeess, the scent of the sea."

"Look outside the window. Any idea where we are?"

"Vlorë?!"

"Yes, love."

On the right side of the road, the gray sea unfolded with rough white waves smashing on the shore full of little stones. I felt the excitement rushing through me and I opened the window all the way down to allow the salty air to caress my face.

"Are we staying in Vlorë, Toni?"

"We are going to stay wherever my princess wishes to."

After a short drive, we couldn't see the sea any longer and had entered a complex with new apartments. We stopped at building number seven.

"Don't tell me you have picked that exact building to stay in," I said suspiciously.

"I am afraid that we are going to stay here," said Toni with some kind of irony.

He parked the car, opened my door, and pulled our luggage out of the car. When we were on the elevator, he put his hands softly around my face and kissed me slowly until the elevator stopped and the doors were about to open. Surprisingly, we stopped on the seventh floor. *Superstitious to the bone*, I thought. He had mentioned once about lucky number seven, but I didn't think he was serious about it and truly believed those kind of things.

The hallway was empty and quiet. With one hand Toni was trying to open the door while his other hand was on my hair and I was pulled close to him. Without waiting for the door to open, he started kissing me, first on my lower lip and then on the upper one in a rhythm that was getting more and more intense. Our breathing got heavier and we couldn't wait to be inside of that apartment. I was so into the moment that I barely noticed what a nice place it was. Our hands were all over each other's bodies, trying to take off our clothes as quickly as possible. Naked finally, with adjacent bodies, whispering lovely words, unleashing whimpering and lustful cries, we made love passionately. It started out slow with sweet, light kisses, our lips making noises from the ecstasy. The things we did I'd never even had the guts to think about before, let alone perform them. I never thought I belonged to that category of women who could make love like that. But I felt relieved, I felt fulfilled, I felt free. I knew that I felt something that I had never felt before, not ever in my life. I felt something so wonderful but frightening at the same time. It was one of those feelings that you're afraid you'll get addicted to instantly. What I could compare to an African safari where all the powerful screams and noises of the different animals are harmonized like a big beautiful choir that gives you chills. This was my jungle, my safari, where I entered fearlessly. One thing was for sure: this place was pulling me in magically, and I was about to experience true love for the first time in my life. If I only knew that the kind of love I was about to experience was the crazy kind. The kind over which wars were started and enemies were made. I felt it deep in my soul that something big was about to happen and my life was going to change forever. I was ready for the mystery and magic to unfold. But did I meet my true love at the wrong time?

I was lying lazily on top of Toni, and at that moment I got up and noticed the neatness of his apartment.

"Oh, how pleasant it is here," I said, looking around at the details now.

Toni got up as well and fixed my hair. The apartment was cottage style, painted a light gray, almost white color and furnished so tastefully. The light color was dominant with some turquoise or blue accessories breaking it up perfectly. Through the open, long, also-white curtains, you could see the balcony with the sea view. Toni was following me around and, once he noticed my curiosity, opened the curtains all the way so I could see the sunset. The sun was already disappearing, leaving behind only some reddish orange stripes mixed with other purple, black, and gray ones.

"Oh, that view is breathtaking!" *Just like the one I have in Miami* almost slipped from my tongue but I decided not to mention it. I had moved there to escape the harsh winters of Chicago. Toni's apartment was exactly how he'd mentioned it in our hourly, long-distance conversations and how I'd pictured it. When I used to describe how I imagined our apartment if we moved in together someday, I was describing exactly the one he already had. He had gone out and rented this one with the hope that I would like it so much I'd never want to leave his place. I felt spoiled, no denying that; I was touched by it all and it teared me up. What good had I done to deserve someone like that? I felt like I was the luckiest woman alive. Thank you, universe! Thank you, God! Thank you, Aphrodite, you love goddess! Thank you, angels, who are helping me in my happiness!

Those short days spent at Toni's place were absolutely the best days of my life. They were simply wonderful and not because we were doing anything spectacular. Just being there in each other's arms—most of the time with no clothes on—was priceless. All we did was drink some good wine, have some long, deep conversations, laugh until our ribs were hurting over crazy, stupid little things. That must have been what they called happiness.

While I would take a short nap, Toni would finish his paperwork that had piled up on his computer. Even after waking up, I would stay lying down while admiring him entirely. I adored him. To me, he was perfection, the man of my dreams, the one I had been waiting for all my life and hadn't met until now. One time when I was lying on my back over Toni's body, while he played with my hair, he whispered me a question.

"How is all this going to go, love?"

I didn't answer right away. I didn't even have an answer for him.

"I don't want to spend a minute away from you, my love. I am not sure if you truly understand how I feel about you," Toni said.

"I do understand, Toni, I do. But what do you want from me? Everything is so complicated and it's almost impossible for us to be with one another..." I couldn't finish my sentence, I felt nauseous. "We don't have a future, Toni, do you understand? We only have the present."

"Stay here with me. Don't go back anymore." He said those words so seriously and I knew he meant them.

I laughed.

"Ah, if only it was that simple, I would have done it in a heartbeat, with no hesitation. We both know how that goes. Once I leave, you will forget about me. Far from the eyes, far from the heart. You will meet other girls. I see how they look at you here. Soon after I will just be somebody that you used to know."

"My heart is held hostage, Ema. That alone makes it impossible for a man to forget the woman that he once loved. By the way, the girls have always been here, last time I checked, but it doesn't matter. My eyes see only you. My heart beats only for you, my love, my everything..."

If I knew at that moment the turn things were going to take in my life, I would have never left that apartment, ever. Even if my life depended on it...

Chapter 3

The past...

To have the ability to love others, to give love, to have that in your heart—it is not necessarily something that you are born with. It is said that it can be taught by example, mainly by your mother. Nature versus nurture. Not for me though. For me, it was totally the opposite. My mother was a cold woman by nature. Either she didn't love anyone or had no clue how to love. She was pretty, serious, and full of secrets. Her confidence gave her a respectful presence. She was very attractive and people would like her instantly without her having to try to win anyone over. That always made me wonder. People not only adored her charm but would feel good in her company.

She had very light-colored, flawless skin, and dark, shoulder-length chestnut hair around her face that made a nice contrast with her skin tone. She had this distinguished, perfect, small nose that might have contributed to her natural confidence. Her lips were full and she would always wear the same classy red lipstick. Her eyebrows were thick, dark, and nicely shaped with a dramatic arch. I remember when my dad was in a good mood, he used to sing a song to her in which the lyrics said, "she killed me with a smile and not a sword. She had big, light brown eyes. She had a beautiful laugh that made her sound so happy. This could fool a lot of people.

She only laughed like that when she was surrounded by people. At home, inside those walls, she would transform into a different creature: something not human, more like a scary, cold, marble statue. It is safe to say that I was terrified of her when she reached that stage sometimes. I used to think that maybe someone else was entering her body and turning her into a demon like the ones I had seen in exorcism movies. It didn't take much to provoke her; even a very small, stupid, unimportant reason could turn her into a monster. I was so terrified by her explosions that I would try to be as careful as I could to avoid those situations. Unfortunately, I wasn't always successful. One time I forgot and left a bowl of soup unwashed somewhere around the house. When my mother found out, she lost it. She turned exactly into that monster I was so terrified of. With her now crazy eyes, she came in my direction and threw the bowl straight at me while calling me all kinds of names. It hit me right in the head before crashing into pieces on the floor. Blood started streaming down from my head and splashed onto some of those pieces of porcelain. Then my mother charged at me and that alone made me straighten up immediately.

"Did you see what you made me do?" she said. "Sit down."

I didn't even dare to breathe at that moment, afraid to upset her any further. Also she seemed to feel sorry. She placed a white piece of gauze on the wound and told me to hold it tight. She didn't kiss me. She didn't apologize, but it was all my fault anyway.

I often wondered why I aggravated her so much. According to her, my clothes were too tight and provocative and my light makeup was unnecessary. In her eyes, I was a free spirit and a rebel child, just like my father. She accused me constantly of being the main reason for my parents' divorce. That was hurtful mostly because she couldn't understand that one of the things I missed the most was having my father around. I would cry myself to sleep that he had left us. The atmosphere was different when he was around. I missed even simple things like his daily routine before he went to work. My favorite of his rituals was the shaving one. He would use the brush to put shaving soap all over his face, and I would watch every move of the shaver as it exposed his now smooth cheeks. Then he would throw shaving cologne on his palms and lightly slap his face. After that, I would follow him to the breakfast table where we ate, and he read the newspaper while we had a conversation. He would ask me about school, about books I'd read, and he would recommend me some others to read. My father would praise me for my good grades constantly and mention how proud he was. I really did only get good grades.

On the other hand, living with my mother was next to impossible. I missed my old house where I had spent some of the best years of my life. We used to live with my grandparents and I missed them dearly. I always believed that my life was a fairy tale thanks to them. They knew how to make me feel special and made my life simply wonderful. I missed their cooking by the wood-burning fireplace. These days fireplaces are mostly for decoration and ambiance, but back home people did their cooking there too. There was a thick metal chain that hung down close to the top of the fire. You could hang a thick pot on that chain when you wanted to cook something there. I would often get lost daydreaming and thinking while I looked at the flames. My cheeks would have two round red spots from the warmth.

The apartment where we lived now was like a fridge. You could get a heart attack from the cold feeling of the sheets when you went to sleep. My room had no heat. We had only one stove in the family room and kitchen that were joined together. Most of the time we would run out of the diesel fuel needed to keep it going; it was expensive and we often had no money. My mother hated being poor, and pretending not to be must have made her feel better.

She'd occasionally mention an old electric heater we had but we couldn't afford to use that either. Many times I'd go to sleep without dinner—if you could even call a piece of dark toasted bread with some butter and a cup of tea dinner. The weight I lost was noticeable, especially since I was thin to begin with.

My grandma, on the other hand, thought I was sad all the time. She used to kiss me on the hair, on my forehead, and give me those long hugs where I would squeeze her tight. She was petite and voluptuous and hugging her gave me the most peaceful feeling. I loved her with all my heart, and felt free and not judged by her. She knew how to point out my best qualities and that had a very positive effect on my broken, insecure, and damaged self-esteem. I didn't feel guilty around her—like I felt around my mother for whom I couldn't do anything right—and I had no fear of anything. She used to give me such a sense of calmness. My grandmother was also my confidante whom I could confess all my problems to or anything that was bothering me at that moment. I could share with her any secret I wanted, from my mother to my friends or boys. She tactfully gave me some of the best advice I ever received that guided and served me my whole life. My grandma was the only person I could trust enough to open up to about my mother. I remember one time I was so frustrated with her and I told my grandma, "I wish you were my mother instead of what God gave me." She put her hand to her mouth to cover the "ahhh" that was escaping and her eyes were wide open.

"What was that?" she asked in a way that told me "you did something wrong,", but without hurting me.

It was the tone in her voice that never allowed you to get mad at her.

"No, my sweetheart, no. Don't say things like that about your mother."

"Nona," I continued because I'd had enough. We called her Nona, which means "grandma" in my language.

"Your mother is a good woman, doll, but she is having a very difficult time now. Do you know how hard it is to raise two teenage daughters with no husband these days? And the poor woman has no one around to help her, not even her family. She is taking the divorce too hard so try to understand her, sweetie. It will pass, hopefully it is just a phase. I don't believe any mother exists who doesn't love her children."

It was strange that she would pick my mother's side when my father was her son. Wasn't she supposed to stand up for him instead? But she was full of love and kindness and that was why she had only good things to say about my mother. On the other hand, my mother had Nona on her list of bad people who had ruined her marriage.

"Oh, Nona! If you only knew how she mistreats me, you would change your mind quickly. I wish you were my mother. My real mother."

"Nooo, love, no. Think about orphans. Do you know what their wish is? To have someone to call mother. It's a privilege."

After all, my Nona was a great storyteller. She would use her intonation to turn even a simple story into a Shakespearean one.

"Have I ever told you the story of the mother's heart?"

Without waiting for my answer, she would start.

"Once upon the time in a city with beautiful buildings and stone-cobbled streets used to live a mother with her son. The woman was a widow and she had to work extra hard to secure a good life for her child. Unfortunately for her, the son grew up to be a troublemaker. He was so bad that one day he decided to kill his mother and sell her heart to a butcher for some money in his pocket. He executed his plan just the way he envisioned it. After the cruel boy put her heart inside a bucket, he ran in a hurry to bring it to the butcher, but suddenly he tripped on a stone and fell to the ground. His knees were all scratched and bloody. The bucket went rolling with him and the lid of the bucket opened and his mother's heart fell out right next to him. He looked at it, and was all mad and angry when he heard a voice: 'Did you get hurt, my son?'

"The boy couldn't believe his ears—it was his mother's voice. How could this happen? How could his mother care after all he had done to her? But a mother's heart always cares and loves unconditionally."

By the time she finished that macabre story of hers, I was in tears and could not be mad with my mother any longer. My grandma's kindness softened and warmed my heart. Her diplomatic way of transmitting valuable messages to me through stories like that would make me calmer and somewhat wiser and more understanding. Her words and her voice would heal my wounded soul. I used to sit on her lap and let her play with my hair while she had her next story ready to tell. I was convinced that she created most of them herself because some were nowhere to be found in books and no one had ever heard of them. I'd ask her, "What book is that from?" because I wanted to have them with me and read them again, but she'd just say, "I don't remember." Her stories were known only in our family circle.

Chapter 4

The present...

"What are you thinking, hon?" said Toni as he tied a big white towel on the side of his hip. He had just gotten out of the shower and steam was still coming off his body. My heart skipped a bit every time I realized how attractive he was, with his olive skin and wet, dark hair combed in the back, and his piercing green eyes. Toni was irresistible in many ways. There I was lying down and following all of his graceful movements: how he put two champagne glasses on the table, how he fixed the towel before it fell. And then there was an interruption; it was a knock on the door. A young boy showed up and delivered the food Toni had ordered. It was from one of the best restaurants in town, and the dishes were all my favorites. I must have mentioned some of them nostalgically during one of our conversations.

"I thought it would be better to eat inside tonight, if you don't mind. This way we'll have each other to ourselves a little longer. How do you like that idea?"

"It's brilliant, like it came straight from my brain."

"What can I say, great minds think alike," he said and his big smile showed his perfectly shaped white teeth.

For me that evening turned into one of the most unforgettable ones and stayed in my memory forever. It seemed like a dream and that everything was coordinated with a magical touch. Being with Toni, the taste of champagne (which put me in such a great mood), and making love. We made love until we were exhausted.

Toni and I didn't like talking about our pasts. I never asked him and he wouldn't volunteer either. But I appreciated the fact that he wouldn't kiss and tell when he briefly made a short summary of his previous love life. He never bashed any of his exes and, to my understanding, I don't think he fell hard for any of them. Maybe I wanted to believe that, and secretly I was kind of jealous. It sounds so absurd, but, wishful thinking, I was hoping he was never madly in love in the past. He used to laugh and jokingly say, "Imagine how I should feel." He was obviously a lot more curious about my life and my past, or at least he was more expressive and would ask all kinds of questions. I didn't have many love stories from my past. I got married really young. I didn't date much. They were more like high school crushes. But then he was curious about my husband. He wanted to know how we'd met, how I felt about him, and why on earth I was risking everything just to be with him. I, of course, hated going into details and rewinding my life.

"Ema, I am sorry that I instigate you like that. Don't get me wrong, I have no right to repudiate that part of your life. It's yours either way. It was important to you and maybe still is, but I need to know a few things."

I didn't say anything but I could sense that something was bothering him.

"Have you ever been with anyone else before me while married? If you did, that's okay. Who am I to judge? Maybe you always wanted to experience love and you're here with me because I was so persistent, or maybe..."

"That's very true," I said. "I couldn't resist your harassments day and night, so one day I decided to get on the plane and take care of this problem in person."

"Ha, ha. I just want to bite your lips right now. Tell me why. Why did you do that?"

"I don't know how to explain my whole life in one simple explanation. I will tell you that my marriage was cracking. My husband and I have been cold to one another for quite a while. At the beginning, I didn't understand what was happening to me. Why my feelings changed. I was numbed, and used to blame myself for working long hours. Another time I thought that it could be age related, when we start wanting less sex, but I was only in my thirties and now my forties. Then I thought of those stories I used to hear about couples losing interest in each other after being together for so many years, and that's the time when you start buying the best lingerie and spending quality time together. But that didn't work, and it made me sad thinking about those couples in their eighties, so in love the same way they were in their first year. So I decided age wasn't the factor and had nothing to do with me losing feelings. I was waiting all these years with the hope that someday we would become one of those lovely couples, but it never happened. Just one day, all of a sudden, all these questions rushed into me. Who am I? What do I want and what don't I want in life? What place in the universe do I fill? Am I happy? How much space do I have in my husband's heart? Does he love me? Do I love him? It comes to a point when you realize that it is you who has changed the most. You're not that spontaneous young girl anymore that goes carelessly wherever fate throws her. You are a woman who knows exactly what is missing from her life and knows precisely what fulfills her. Apparently, on the surface, it looks like I have everything good going in my life. People call me lucky. My lifestyle is admired by many, but the reality is that I am always missing something. I don't know what exactly. It's very abstract and sometimes it's a feeling that I have never felt before, and sometimes it feels like destiny. That missing piece of the puzzle somehow might be very important because it could hold the key to my happiness. And then the most terrifying thought, that plays in your mind constantly: 'What if I married the wrong man?' I am married to someone who doesn't know me, who has never bothered to travel to the labyrinths of my soul. I wonder how he'd describe me if asked. Does he know my likes or dislikes? I doubt it. I'm just a trophy for his collection. Take notes, *'Mon Chéri.'* If you ever decide to get married, marry someone that you can talk to for long hours without getting tired of it, because that's what you're going to do for most of your life."

"Thanks for the advice, *'Mon Amour,'* but I know exactly who is going to be the one I'd share my life with," said Toni, who seemed to have enjoyed my confession.

"As for your other question, if I ever had someone before you while married, the answer is no. Doesn't mean that I wasn't tempted, but I never acted on it. I thought having an affair was all wrong until I met you."

"Who knew that I was worth something, huh?" he teased me.

"With you it's different, Toni. I have no explanation why, it just is. I know that I have thrown values and morals out the window. I have broken every rule. I know that all of this is a crazy thing, but for the first time in my life I will follow my heart. After all, I can't stop that even if I wanted to."

Toni kissed me slowly and with admiration. It was one of those kisses that only he knew how to give. The kind that penetrated deep into your soul and you felt them with every cell of your body. I was madly in love with him, I knew that with my whole heart. Maybe he was the one I was missing all my life—this was my destiny. It sounded cliched but now that I had found him, I could never live without him. He was my soul mate, no doubt.

Love and finding your soul mate should be considered the most important thing in a human's life. We are cynics when it comes to love. Money and success are things that we could easily secure, but that not kind of happiness. It rarely happens and only if you're lucky. It is something worth fighting for, something worth every sacrifice. The problem is that, if you don't take risks, you only sabotage yourself, and you will have risked the most important thing in life: your own happiness...

The days I was spending with my lover—because that's what he was, what else could I call him?—had regenerated me. Not only was I sweeter and nicer than ever before, but I was also a lot more generous as well. I was giving money away to every beggar we saw. I must have had a contagious smile on my face because everyone was smiling back at me when we passed.

Every day Toni had a different surprise for me. I was his tourist and he was my tour guide.

Today we were going to visit Rozafa's castle, and after that we were going to sleep somewhere close by in the Alps, probably Theth. There is nothing like the air in the Swiss Alps; it is so fresh, so crisp. Nature is virginal and beautiful. And the food, like they say in America, is "to die for."

"That sounds terrific," I said to him when he suggested it. "I want to go there." I kissed him on both cheeks. "I know about the legend associated with that castle but I have never been there."

"I am glad to take you there for the first time. My princess has seen most of the world but not this castle." He wrapped his arms around me, held me tight, and kissed me on my lips. He put my face between his palms and kissed me again.

"We can leave now," he said. "And you don't need to bring much stuff with you."

"Okay, let me quickly pack some toiletries and we will go."

In literally five minutes I was ready and we jumped in the car. Toni's one hand was at the wheel and the other was holding my hand. I put my head on his shoulder. The aroma of the masculine shampoo he used, mixed with his scent, really stimulated something in me. I liked to smell him. He had no jacket on and only wore a T-shirt. I pulled on his sleeve and pressed my lips against his skin.

"You taste soo good, Toni."

I started to kiss him everywhere—his forearms, his hands, his fingers. One of them I kissed and then sucked it in a provocative way. He pulled my hair and started kissing me hard. Then he released me but I was already out of control. I put my fingers through his hair and kissed him on his neck, his face, his shoulders and was about to jump in his lap. I don't know how quickly all this accelerated to such a crazy, impulsive desire. My eyes were half-closed, my lips were a little bit open, and my breathing had fallen into a hard rhythm.

"You are a little beast. Can you hold on to it? We can't pull over." Toni's eyes were sparkling with desire. I think he liked it that I had lost my control.

"How far are we? No, I can't wait. I will sit on your lap while you drive. Can you drive like that?"

It must have looked like a scene from a movie. Toni laughed and gave me some deadly kisses. Then he unleashed some voices and whispered sweet little threats to prepare me for what was going to happen to me once we arrived at the hotel. Every part of me felt every part of him. Everything he did or said, his gestures, his touch, would make me lose control and melt to a hot liquid that entered his body and so we became one. He must have felt the same and mentioned once before that he wanted to eat me up and have me inside his tummy. I reminded him that I would be pleased if he kept me in his heart. Toni made me feel free. My hormones were running wild and the dopamine rushed through my brain like gasoline through the engine of a car. It was hot, explosive, and exciting.

The trip was a few hours long but I didn't even feel the time passing with him. Hours felt like only minutes and would fly by quickly. It made me sad that those moments would be over soon and that my staying here on the other side of the world was coming to an end. Soon I would go back to reality. Here I felt like I had slid into a magic place or like I was dreaming everything and that, once I woke up, the magic would be gone.

"We're here, my love."

Toni opened the door for me and, with a charming gesture, held my hand to help me get out.

Rozafa's castle was on the top of a high hill, which looked like a giant rock. It was right before you entered the old city of Shkodra. It was built in Illyrians' times and got its name sometime during medieval times. What made that particular castle famous, and a tourist attraction, was the legend associated with it. The legend had to do with the importance of keeping a promise even when it requires extreme sacrifices, like being walled in. When we came close to the entrance, I noticed the small crowd waiting to be directed. Since it wasn't tourist season, there weren't many people around. The tour guide asked us to gather closer because he was about to start telling the story, or the best version of it, according to him. His noticeably strong Northern dialect made it even more interesting. I remember how much I used to like the sound of that accent...

A thick fog covered all of Buna and its surroundings for three days and three nights. The strong winds pushed the fog onto the hill of the Valdanuzit. And there, right on top of the hill, three brothers were working. They were building a castle, but the walls they built during the day were getting destroyed during the night and they couldn't finish it. One day an old man passed by and asked them how their day was. The brothers told him the truth. The old man said that he knew one way how to help them keep those walls standing. The brothers begged him desperately to share his secret with them.

"Are you married?" he asked them.

"Yes, we are," they answered.

"You have to make a promise that you won't share with your wives what I will tell you. One of your wives will come here tomorrow to

27

bring you lunch as usual. The one who comes must be walled inside the castle. After that, this castle will never be destroyed and shall stand tall for centuries to come."

Those were his last words and he disappeared into the fog. The older brother couldn't stand not telling his wife the secret and told her not to show up tomorrow. The second brother did the same thing, except for the youngest one. He kept his mouth shut and only hoped his beautiful wife would not be the one to bring them lunch. He looked sadly at his son, who was just a baby, but still didn't break his promise. Early in the morning, the brothers left for work. They were breaking stones with angry and heavy hearts. At home, the mother of the brothers didn't know what was going on. When the food was ready, she filled the baskets and asked the oldest daughter-in-law to go and bring the meal to the boys.

"Ah, Mother, today I can't. My leg is hurting."

Then she asked the middle one. She complained about her severe headache. Now only the young Rozafa was left to go. She was so innocent and asked all the women to take care of her son while she was gone. She kissed her son and left to go meet the brother on the top of the hill. They looked anxiously at the silhouette approaching.

"How are y'all doing?" she asked. "I brought you food and water. I bet you're hungry."

No one said a word. Their hearts were pounding and their faces were pale. The younger brother fell onto his knees, threw his hammer away, and screamed in pain for the fate and what was about to happen to his kind wife. He cursed her fate, his fate, the castle. His wife went close to him and tried to calm down her husband, who cried uncontrollably, without understanding why. The other brothers told her the truth. She listened and took the news with dignity. She got pale and was about to faint but said, "That is my fate and what is meant to be it will be." She didn't go against it, she didn't scream, but went and laid down next to the wall where they placed her. She was alive while they started putting heavy stones on top of her and mud to make them stick to one another. When she started feeling the weight crushing her and was half walled in, she thought about her son, who would grow up without her and might someday be looking for his mother. He would come right here.

"Stop!" she screamed. "I have one last wish to make. I want you to leave my right eye out, my right hand out, and my right breast and leg as well. I have a baby son at home and I want to see him with my eye, comfort him with my hand, feed him with my breast, and use my leg to shake his crib when he wants to sleep."

They fulfilled her wish. The walls of the castle were never destroyed again and, even today, they are covered with leaves still wet from the tears of Rozafa. Also, around the castle was a creek that was whitish in color from the lead in that area that, according to the legend, is her breast milk.

When the guide finished his story, there was some enthusiastic hand clapping. I was in tears. Toni took my hand and pulled me closer to him as we left the place.

"That Rozafa story was so sad. What a painful legend. Just like our history. It used to have the same effect on me when I was younger but today it makes more sense. It is traumatizing to believe that the people you care the most about are the ones who hurt you," I said and put my arm through his arm.

"Don't you see how we haven't changed at all? We hurt those who love us."

"Those are messages, Toni, passed through generations. They are warnings from our ancestors and life lessons."

"So what is a message that you've got, darling?"

"Hmmm, for a start, life is far more valuable than a stupid promise. Idealizing those kinds of things or religions has its own dangerous consequences."

"Interesting. Go ahead, continue."

"It makes me wonder if it's in our DNA."

"What do you mean by that?"

"It makes me think of some patterns throughout history. What idealizing has done to our people. The latest perfect case is communism. The loyalty of people to that ideology always amazed and terrified me at same time. We ended up in self-isolation from the rest of the world, creating our own hell and destruction. The worst part was that we were in denial, wouldn't get it, wouldn't admit that we failed. That ideology was a hoax."

"Do you want to hear what lesson I got from all this, Ema?"

"Totally, love."

"You have to lose something in order to gain something. That was one, the other one is: to hell with the castle, you can live happy in a hut if you are with the person that you love."

"Ah, that's not very realistic in today's world. In fact, another lesson and message comes into my mind at this moment."

"Which is?"

"In life you can't have everything. And that's the most proven, true statement in life."

Toni pulled me toward him with his hands around my shoulders and said, looking me straight in the eyes, "You will have everything, my princess."

We walked quietly around other parts of the castle. For a moment, it felt like someone had thrown cold water on me to wake me up and bring me back to reality. This wasn't real. This was a fantasy. Somewhere far away I had a family. I was a mother, a devoted one. I was a wife, a good one, up until not too long ago at least. My devotion to my family was finished, was done. I was dipped in sin. I was an adulteress. I had broken the promise "'til death do us part." I was rebelling and derailing. Satan was my guide; he had convinced me that my unlimited freedom was something far more important than my morals and family values. But to my surprise, I was fearless. Nothing could scare me or stop me from doing what I felt was right for me, for my soul. As a lover, I would be rewarded with a prize. I crossed oceans and left everything behind just to spend a few passionate nights with the one I loved. I thought he was the love of my life, the ONE, and the only one to ever make me feel the way I felt. I gave 100 percent in everything I did and loved. I had done the same thing for my family before. It was no accident that my daughter was one of the top students in school. She was a good girl, an easygoing child who made us proud all the time. People would say she was a mirror of me. As a spouse, I was a very responsible one. I never abused our finances even though we were in great shape financially. I kept only two cleaning ladies for the mansion we lived in. Also, I had a maintenance company who took care of the gardening and the swimming pool. But that was all. I could afford all kinds of extra stuff, like a butler, or other live-in servants, but I didn't. I enjoyed cooking healthy delicious meals for my family regardless of my busy schedule. I considered myself a good wife, and Toni not only agreed with me but was wondering why I was even questioning myself. When we made the decision to enter into our relationship, he would insist that sometimes the things that seemed wrong could be the right ones. I would come up with clichéd, moralistic arguments that came from my guilty conscience, and he would have the right, convincing answers for me. He thought that the more we tried to avoid and deny our feelings for each other, the more damage we would do to our souls. We were going to be the ones to suffer the consequences for the sake of some stupid rules and to keep everyone else happy. Those were the things we were discussing walking around the castle, and at the end I told him, "I am not Rozafa."

He laughed and said, "I'm not the little brother either, I am the middle one. It's a fact..."

Chapter 5

That day we walked around everywhere exploring that mystic place. We had dinner in a restaurant built right at the corner where two high mountains met. It was all made of wood and was surrounded by high trees. Not far from it was a small waterfall that would break the quietness of the place. At night, we stayed on the hotel's balcony for a little while to enjoy the tranquility mixed with the noises of nature. I thought I heard a wolf howling in the distance. It was more than one, maybe a pack of them. Toni said, from what he knew of the place, that it was the territory of wolves and grizzly bears. People carried guns with them when they walked around, and farmers protected their sheep with aggressive Rottweilers. Not the kind you kept as pets but the less domesticated ones whose specific purpose was to kill when sheep were in danger.

It got chilly and we had to go inside. I sat by the huge fireplace built with big stones from the local rivers. The fire was so beautiful and warm and I have always loved the scent of burning wood. We sipped a good wine and that alone made those deep conversations even better. We made love until morning with our bodies curled up with one another. When I woke up in the morning, for a moment I couldn't figure out where I was. Then I saw Toni's arm wrapped around me. I didn't move because I didn't want to ruin that beautiful moment. My lips felt sore and I swallowed more than usual. I could taste him all over me, on my lips, on my body, inside me. He was sleeping so peacefully with his head against the white pillow. The reflection of his dark, black-bluish hair against his skin made him irresistible. Oh God, he was so handsome. But what drew me toward him the most was his soul, his beautiful soul. Everything I had ever wanted or looked for in a man I had found in him. He was lying next to me and he was mine and mine only. I was so happy that tears of joy rolled down from my eyes. But in the meantime I was also so sad as I cuddled up against his warm chest...

We asked for breakfast to be served in our room. The enthusiasm of the night before had left us and we couldn't believe how fast those days had gone by. One more day and I would go back where I came from. I felt powerless, weak, almost sick, and let myself lean on him while sipping my coffee quietly. Toni instinctively played with my hair. He would kiss my forehead, my nose, my cheeks, my lips. Then he would squeeze me tightly like I was about to disappear right at that moment. He whispered constantly how much he loved me.

"How am I going to live without you, my love? Tell me how. I won't be able to function. My lungs are hurting like someone is pulling them out." His eyes were teary.

"Oh, my love. You will fall in love again. You deserve the best girl in the world. I'm not for you, Toni. You know things like this don't fly easily around here. We would have the world against us."

"Ah, my heart. What you're saying is hurtful. I couldn't love anybody else. You are the best for me and I can feel that if I lose you, I will never ever love like this again. You have no idea how I feel about you."

His tears rolled down his cheeks and so did mine. I couldn't get enough air, I couldn't breathe.

"Please stay with me, Ema. Don't go back. I love you! I love you more than you'll ever know."

I was kissing his tears and letting mine run like a river as I said to him, "I love you more, my love, my everything, I love you more. You should come to me. Can you? I don't want to live without you either."

"I will, my heart. I will never lose you. That's the best solution, me going there."

"But, Toni, you have an established life here. You just got promoted to a higher position. I don't want to ruin your life."

"You think my job is more important than being with you, Ema?"

"I don't want to make promises I can't keep. My divorce will take time and I could never live with you prior to that being over with."

"You don't have to worry about that. I can survive as long as I have you close and am able to see you when you can."

"What if you get tired of waiting for me? America, it changes people. Money becomes an important thing; it's a different world over there."

"Ema, you're the one I've been waiting all my life to meet. I would turn the world upside down to be with you and make you mine..."

The entire last day we spent at the hotel and never left the room, not even to grab something to eat. Our appetite was gone anyway. I was melancholic and annoying while Toni would calm me down with his promise that very soon he would meet me in Chicago. Leaving the airport was the hardest part. They say airports have seen more kisses and promises than wedding altars. We were standing in each other's arms without moving, just feeling our coordinated heartbeats with the hope that they would continue to beat the same across the distance.

"I promise you, my love, that very soon I will be there, remember that. I love you, my sweet angel, my beautiful girl, love of my life."

"I love you more, Toni..."

Switzerland was the transit country where I had to wait for my connecting flight to Chicago. A snowstorm was coming and many flights were canceled, including mine. I decided to spend the night at one of the hotels close by. I sent my daughter Ina a text message to notify her of the delay. I told her she could call me anytime if she wanted to. I called Ben, and my stomach was turning upside down from guilt. He hadn't called me once during my time away, probably thinking I was so busy working, not to mention the time change. It wouldn't be fair to be mad at him. By nature, he was cold and indifferent. My sister would mention that every chance she'd get when I used to take his side, justifying him. He was a workaholic. If he wasn't on the phone, he would be on the computer working.

When I called, a girl who, from her voice, didn't sound like she was more than twenty picked up the phone.

"Hellooo," she said in a singsong voice.

"Hi, who is this?"

"Ouch, oh shoot," she said and hung up the phone.

I called again and this time Ben picked up. Without asking me how I was doing first, he went straight into apologizing for the situation.

"Honey, it is not how it looks. She is my secretary..."

"Ben, no need to apologize. Stop. I had no idea your secretary was that young."

"She is not that young, only a few years younger than you."

"Please stop. I just called to let you know my flight is canceled. That's all."

I felt betrayed somehow, but that whole deal did release me from my guilty conscience. I had no desire to ask him questions nor did I care. What was happening with me, Ben, us in general? How had our family ended up like this? How did we get to this point? The right answer, at that moment, would be that our marriage had been over for a while. We were simply living comfortably in the misery we had created for each other. We just didn't have the guts to admit with honesty the compromise we had made for living a lie.

I cried my eyes out for at least an hour with my head dropped on my pillow. I felt empty and lonely. I was missing everyone. I missed my Ina, my wonderful girl who always had the best head on her shoulders. She was so mature at such a young age and could see everything with transparency. We were very similar yet very different. I had a tendency to overdramatize or overromanticize things. She was more realistic, precise, firm, grounded, black and white, not gray. I was a mixture of colors; I would put question marks when a period was needed instead. I missed Toni, who always had the right answer and gave me the peace I needed. I missed Ben, who made my life feel secure. He taught me that if I carefully played that big game called life, I could achieve anything I wanted. He had made me believe that fate was in our hands, at least for the most part.

I felt like everyone was leaving me. I was trying to remember fragments from Ben's behavior lately. How long might he have had a lover on the side? Maybe around the same time when he got himself a new Porsche 911 Turbo S. I thought it was completely unnecessary. In total he had six exotic cars and one small yacht. He would joke that all he needed now to be complete was a small plane. He went and got his pilot license. I swore I would never fly with him. All of those things I associated with a man's midlife crisis and he was at that age now, mid-forties. I thought he was working more than ever because he would come home late in the evening every day. I thought he was traveling more often for business lately too. A long time ago he used to beg me to go on those business trips and we would call them mini vacations, but not lately. People change gradually through the years and sometimes that change goes unnoticed. Only when circumstances change do we realize who we are and who the people we share our reality with are. We start noticing things that weren't there before or maybe we ignored them.

Ben had become more arrogant than usual. As a result of this behavior, he had secured enough enemies, some involved with his business as well. I don't think he had any true friends, mostly acquaintances. Those were the ones he called friends, but their only connection was through work and contracts. They were divided into categories; some were more important than others. He would gather with the important ones once in a while to smoke a cigar, drink old whiskey, and play poker. The important ones were mostly investors. Childhood friends or the ones from school were nonexistent; he had no connection with them. I never understood why they were distant from him to that point. He thought they were envious and jealous of his success.

"I don't need them," he would say. "They are useless to me like a tree with no fruit. All they want from me is money and favors, I don't need them."

He didn't trust anyone. I, on the other hand, was so busy running everything else—work, family, my daughter, school, and everyone's well-being. No question I might have changed too, possibly a lot. If living in luxury was something I wasn't familiar with in the past, now I had grown accustomed to it. That was my new norm and I couldn't imagine my life any differently. We lived in a gated community, with multimillion-dollar mansions. I couldn't imagine living anywhere else now, without a security guard to open the gates and give me that peace of mind for our safety. I couldn't imagine my daughter attending any public school, only private and top-rated ones.

When we built our house a few years ago, I wanted the ceilings to be higher than standard. I begged Ben by making puppy dog faces, and told him I couldn't breathe otherwise. He reminded me that I must have forgotten how and where I was raised that now a regular mansion didn't have enough oxygen for me. My cheeks burned from the embarrassment I felt. It was said in a mean way, but it didn't surprise me. The space between us grew bigger every day. He did his things and I did mine. I never asked questions or interfered with his life.

Toni was right when he mentioned once that water can't enter the boat if it has no cracks in it. He was convinced that nothing could break a strong relationship, nothing. It was obvious that our marriage had its cracks that had been opening for a while now. It was done, over, finished, dead. We were simply two people living under same roof, roommates. I talked to Toni that night until my eyelids were getting heavy. With his conversation he'd fill my heart with love and admiration. I kept falling deeper and harder for him, for his kindness and honesty. I felt lucky and fulfilled for the first time in my life...

Chapter 6

I had been back in Chicago for a few days. The situation at home was tense. I was barely talking to Ben and I was avoiding him. He tried to apologize and make ridiculous excuses about that girl who picked up the phone. I asked him to keep our daughter out of our stupid, immature arguments. Things were more serious than I had imagined. Totally by accident, while looking for something and going through bank statements, I found large amounts of dollars transferred to checking accounts that were only in his name and that I wasn't aware even existed. What was he doing behind my back? I confronted him with what I'd found but then regretted it because not only wasn't he truthful about it but then he gave me a twisted version of what was really going on. He got aggravated and raised his voice to shut down any attempt of me investigating him further.

His phone was ringing quite often at any hour of the day and night, all calls from that girl. He yelled at her too and asked her to never call again. Our relationship was so over that nothing bothered me anymore; nothing like that would get on my nerves. We were both guilty of cheating on each other and the only thing keeping us together was our daughter and our investments. Ina was grown up enough to hopefully understand that divorce for us was not only inevitable but necessary. It was not fair for both of us to hold each other hostage to the misery we had created. In the end we both deserved to be happy.

When I finally asked Ben for a divorce, he cursed everything from his life to me and started pointing fingers. He blamed me for ruining his life, our family, our daughter's life, our future. He was counting all his sacrifices and I wasn't mentioned once on that long journey of togetherness. I wasn't given any credit for being in the "First Wives Club."

The next morning, when he was calmer and in a better mood, he apologized and made a sincere request to give our marriage another chance and try to save it.

"Oh, Ben. I would forgive anything—wrong investments, gambling..." I didn't mention alcoholism but I did think it and I had to bite my tongue to hold it in. "But I would never forgive betraying, cheating. What is it they say, if you're torn between two lovers, always choose the second one. If you loved the first one, there wasn't ever going to be a second one. You made your choice very clear, Ben. Keep chasing that young girl of yours; don't lose her for as long as you still have money in your hands."

Ben looked crushed. I had never seen him like that.

"Ema, she means nothing to me."

I rolled my eyes to let him know that our conversation was over.

"Anyway, whatever rocks your boat, Ema. Get a lawyer and I have a feeling we're going to have a very long divorce process."

"Not necessarily. It only takes a few months if we agree to fairly share our assets."

"Exactly," he said, giving the impression that he wasn't going easy on that. "Can I ask you for a favor?"

"Shoot," I said.

"I don't want Ina to know. We have to find the right time to tell her. Her world will be turned upside down and she has no fault in that. She should not suffer for our mistakes."

"Why are you making it seem like this is all my fault, Ben? Where were you when I was feeling left alone to take care of her, of our family?"

"I was out busting my ass working day and night to give you a good life. But you were dripping in luxury without even paying attention to how the money was coming in. It was never enough, Ema. No matter what I did, it was never enough for you."

"I was alone, Ben. Alone in my bed, alone vacationing with my daughter, alone watching TV. For years my heart was craving to have a husband who was my best friend so we could share conversations together, random ones, ordinary ones. But you were always busy, if not with work, you were out drinking in clubs with your friends. Who knows, maybe you always had someone else on the side?"

"Where was I? I was there at the dinner table to be with my family but you couldn't stand how I ate or how I chewed and swallowed my food. So I started having meals by myself so you could enjoy yours in peace. I liked it too because I allowed myself to eat any way I wanted, chewing loudly, licking my fingers. As for bed, when we used to sleep together. You would make me leave the room because my snoring was so loud, like a polar bear, remember? That was the nickname you baptized me with. I started sleeping in the guest room, so you could have your beauty sleep uninterrupted. I was there to talk to you but you hated my taste in music and I am clueless when it comes to art. According to you, I am arrogant, controlling, possessive, and I make you blush in front of your elite friends. All I have is money, the only valuable thing. I remember what you said during one of our heated arguments like it was yesterday: if you really want to know the value of a person, strip him of his success and money and see what he has left. Is he worth being with? I did this in my mind quietly, Ema. I was going to choose you over and over again, like the most beautiful, intelligent, so worth keeping woman that you are. But I am sure you wouldn't do the same for me. You wouldn't choose me."

Ben left the room, slamming the door, and I dropped onto the couch, exhausted...

Chapter 7

The past...

When you go back to your home country after more than a decade, your first desire is to explore places you're familiar with and have to do with your past. Many things have changed and many have stood the test of time. Everything I saw—a narrow street where I used to walk daily, a neighbor now older and gray-haired, a park, a tree with lovers' initials carved into it—made me nostalgic. Those little things brought back a lot of memories and I missed the time that had passed by. I missed those people who I had almost forgotten existed and who all of a sudden had invaded my memory. Right outside the building I grew up in was a new coffee shop. If you hung around there long enough, you had a good chance of meeting pretty much everyone you knew. It was the biggest socializing place in the neighborhood. What caught my eye was that there were noticeably many more of them popping up, like mushrooms, all over the town. Supposedly this was considered one of the changes, investments of this kind. People would whisper their owners' names, some of them involved in government, using those shops for money laundering. Strong emotions were running through me when I entered the stairs of the building to get to my old apartment. I had run up and down those stairs millions of times and one vivid memory came through...

I'm not sure if being a pretty girl is always a blessing. It could be a curse instead. Being a pretty girl, with all the perfection that nature had created, mixed with a sensual nature, can also be a deadly combination, or, even worse yet, can be dangerous. At least that's how it worked in this sleepy town of mine. Because once you step foot outside your home, you enter into a jungle. A jungle with horny boys who liked to prey on attractive girls. To them this was the entertainment of the day, and for some women that sparked jealousy. Being closed-minded, and I would add, mean hearted without hesitation, those women saw pretty girls as a personification of sin. That alone would give them reason to judge every move they made and every behavior to see if something was inappropriate, according to their standards, so they could use it later, in case they chose to. Bad-mouthing them and making up stories was pure entertainment. Their days would be fulfilled if they had enough material to justify unleashing all the anger and misery developed during their hard lives.

"Did you see her black eye? They didn't let her in. She slept on the stairs all night long. Agimi almost tripped over her when he left for work."

"Was she sleeping on the floor? Oh, poor girl."

This was their talk, showing how sorry they felt when they found out that a pretty girl had slept on the floor, outside her home. But it was all fake and an act. The truth was they hated her. The best part, when the excitement started, was when they learned more information and more details came to the surface. Their sensors sharpened and their vicious investigation started.

Meli was a beautiful sixteen-year-old who wasn't aware what she possessed. With her almost naive nature, but a bit of a rebellious personality, she didn't care much for anything. Meli would spend most of the day outside either playing soccer with the boys or daydreaming, sitting on the stairs in front of her apartment.

Her mother passed away when she was just a little girl, leaving her in the care of her father and her brothers. All of them worked long hours in factory shifts, so basically she was alone for most of the day and could do whatever she wanted. She didn't like school that much and she'd skip classes any chance she got. Rumors were that she was pregnant and that could be the reason why her brothers beat her up so badly and then kicked her out of the house. It was the right thing for her brothers to do in response to the dishonor she had brought to their family. Those thin walls let all the curious neighbors hear when she was screaming like crazy and yelling that it wasn't her fault. Through her tears she hysterically told them what had happened to her.

"He tied me up. He closed my mouth. He put his gun to my head," she shouted, but her words fell on deaf ears. She cursed and said all those crazy things about Shefik. She cursed her brothers for not believing her. She cursed her own fate. Her brothers didn't care what she had to say. Obviously not only did they not believe her but they still blamed her for spending all day on the stairs. Logically for them, it was like she asked for this to happen. All the neighbors heard it. Those thin walls had ears that were anxiously trying to catch every hint of the story.

I heard it too. I believed Meli. I might have been the only one who believed her. There was something very convincing in her voice and in the way she explained things, but that at the same time were useless to say because no one was listening to her. To be honest, Shefik always gave me the creeps when we'd run into each other on the building stairs. I was a very young girl but it would give me a weird vibe the way he'd look at me. Shefik was a man maybe in his early fifties, married and with two children. He always wore this army uniform and neighbors called him "General." This nickname was given out of respect because not only was he working for the government but he also held some kind of high position.

People viewed him as someone important, someone whose good side you better be on. People were forced to respect him.

The hypocrisy of communism was like that with equality. It appeared that all citizens were supposedly equal in the eyes of each other and that social status didn't have any meaning or any value. As result, everyone lived a very simple life and it didn't matter if you were a professor or a scientist, a shoemaker or a factory worker, you lived in the same tiny apartments the government provided, styled all with same decor and furniture. It all seemed like it functioned harmoniously, but the reality is that human nature was not wired to work like that. Even in a communist regime where wealthy people do not exist, there are different ways to show power and inequality. Someone working for the government or the Communist Party was seen as someone trusted by them and had that unsaid status of superiority. People also feared "the important" ones. It was a law of nature, or of the jungle. Eat or be eaten.

Shefik had that kind of power over the other paupers in his building. They might all live in same environment with the same standards but no one had the privileges under the table like he did. According to Meli, one day when everyone had left for work or school on their daily routines, she decided to take a day off from school as she often did. She liked to just wander around every once in a while and do absolutely nothing. Shefik was off that day as well and when he saw her hanging around, he asked for her help. He asked her nicely to help him in his apartment. Without thinking twice, Meli followed him inside. Why wouldn't she when he was the most respected and important man in the building? Once she was inside, Shefik closed the door, took the key out, and threw it in his pocket. Meli thought that was kind of odd and something instinctive made her feel not right about it. Then it got worse when he directed her into his bedroom.

"That's where I need your help," he said. But why did he look so different, she wondered. Shefik's face was all red, like a turkey's wattle, and his cheeks were burning like he had some kind of high fever. He started coming toward her and when he got too close, he said, "I would never tell anyone what is about to happen. You should do the same, understand? Do you know how much I like you? I have spent all this time thinking of your perky boobs. Those thoughts keep me awake at night, you know."

Then he grabbed Meli's hand and pulled her closer. She tried to leave, panicked, and warned him, "Let me go. I will scream so hard that everyone will hear."

But with a quick maneuver, he had twisted her arm and turned her over while covering her mouth. With his other hand, he had pulled out his gun and placed it to her head. Shefik told her that one more move and he would blow her brains out and make her disappear.

"No one will come looking for you, because you're nothing but a little whore that fucked every boy in town." Then he went to kiss her.

Meli was trying to keep herself from throwing up from his stinking presence. He must not have showered in weeks and his breath smelled like something had died inside his mouth. The more she resisted, the more aggressive and excited he became. He punched her hard in the stomach, leaving her struggling to breathe while he ripped her underwear and forced himself inside her like crazy. Meli was crying, terrified, and, for a moment, she thought would suffocate, but Shefik had lost it by now from her resistance and punched her hard again in her stomach. Now she truly couldn't breathe and crumbled from the pain. He took advantage of the situation and placed duct tape over her mouth and handcuffed her to the metal rails of his bed. Now that she was powerless and completely under his control, he raped her rapidly, panting like an animal, until he had no energy left. When he was done and finished, he had this satisfied look on his face. It made him feel powerful and like he had achieved something different this time. Shefik thought she had enjoyed it and that resisting was part of the game girls played, especially those little inexperienced ones. He even had the guts to act nicely to her and suggested to Meli that they could do this often and that this lovemaking game could be their little secret. But if she opened her mouth and said even one word to someone, she would be found dead in any creek or thrown on the side of the road like a whore. Also he threatened he'd hurt her brothers and send them to working camps.

"No one would believe you, Melina girl, no one," he said, calling her the name only those closest to her would.

Meli didn't tell anyone. Shefik was right. No one would believe her and she couldn't ruin her brothers' lives. It was her fault for staying on the stairs all day and catching the eyes of predators. She didn't hang out there any longer and barely left the house. She had that sick-looking, sad face now and her body was getting rounder and heavier every day. Her brothers looked at her suspiciously. They weren't happy with the way she was changing every day. Meli couldn't take it anymore and decided to confess to her older brother. She waited for him until he came home from his night shift at work. The whole neighborhood was up that night. You could hear a fight in progress, a physical and bad one. They were probably throwing Meli on the couch or smashing her into the walls because she was screaming in pain. We all heard it but no one came to her rescue. That's how it was, like a code; everyone minds their own business when it comes to domestic abuse or violence. I felt sorry for poor Meli. Not only did I believe her, but I knew that whatever happened was exactly how she described it. I was too young to interfere even if I wanted to, but mentally I showed solidarity with her. Bad news travels quicker. Now everyone was talking about her. They would give their lame opinions to put some kind of justice in place. To my surprise, they would take Shefik's side, even women.

"Can you believe that? That little whore would spread those shameful rumors about an honorable man like Comrade Shefik. To be that young and with such a devilish dirty mind, it's scary. She should be burned like witches on a wooden pyre. She is not like every other regular girl, she is the devil. Her poor family had to deal with her, and she brought shame to them..."

Meli left her home after that and never returned. No one ever asked for her either; no one really cared. Years later when communism fell and the borders were open, she escaped to Greece. Her son at that time had grown to be five or six years old.

Meli's story brought back some memories from the past, which I had forgotten. Her story had no direct connection with my life but, along with many others, had somewhat influenced the direction I would take toward the profession I chose. It wasn't totally by accident that I chose to be a psychologist and that my career revolved around abused women. I felt like that profession chose me...

Chapter 8

The past...

Traveling by trains was the most common form of transportation those days because there wasn't any other alternative. During the communist era, people weren't allowed to own cars and the government only provided their limited number of old run-down trains and buses for traveling. Adults seemed to hate those trips; they complained about how long and exhausting they were. They would leave at 5:00 a.m. for the only train station, which was far away from where people lived. So you had to wake up really early and walk a long way to finally sit on those old, dirty seats. The train itself stank from the heavy air created by the mixture of people's sweat and the homemade food they had packed with them. The places where you could grab a coffee or a sandwich were nonexistent. "A true horror," that was what my mother would say. As for me, except for the fact that I had to get up early, I didn't mind at all. I would follow her with one eye open and one eye closed, all sleepy, but once I was inside the train, I would get comfortable on the seat and really enjoyed those trips. I never complained. To me they were like an interesting adventure. I was amazed at how quickly we would cross cities and farms, leaving them behind. I would imitate instinctively the monotone rhythm of the wheels on the tracks and would get all excited when the dimmed lights of the train would turn on when it entered those pitch-black tunnels inside a mountain. That was the moment I would see the reflection of the other passengers in the window. Some were sleeping and some were conversing with one another.

I would get lost in my thoughts when, at slower speeds, I would see women washing clothes by the river and kids with sheep and cows lying in the grass. I imagined myself being born in one of those villages. I probably would have had my own cow to take care of, to feed her grass or lie back against her belly reading a book like I had seen in some paintings. The best part was when the train would stop in different cities to drop off some passengers and take on others. Outside the station were farmers, mostly teenagers with dirty hair from the dust of the road and skin already dark and wrinkled from staying too long in the sun. They would carry baskets of seasonal fruits and yell loudly, competing with each other to market and sell their produce. One time my mother and I were tempted to get some figs, which were the best tasting ones I've ever had. It didn't make sense to be there and not bring a basket of fresh figs home. While we were paying for them, the train started to leave and was about to pick up speed any minute. I will never forget the adrenaline and panic we felt at that moment. We were mostly afraid that my hand would slip from hers and that we'd get separated. We rushed inside and promised each other we'd never do that again. Who cared about figs and peaches? They weren't worth the stress.

During lunchtime there was a different wave of scents coming through the air, a mixture of strong garlic and onions or boiled eggs. My mother was about to throw up while I still wasn't bothered. Passengers were very kind and would offer or exchange things with each other, including us. Some of the cookies they offered looked delicious and I wanted to try them but that would go against what my mother had told me prior to the start of the trip: to never accept anything offered by strangers even if I was dead hungry, and not to give any explanation or information about us to curious people. I would sit quietly like I wasn't there and, in my own world, enjoy the trip on my own way.

Here and there I would get interested in their conversations, or their raw emotions when they would tell stories. I had come to the conclusion that people who were traveling on those trains were very superstitious and that the destinations they were going to had something to do with some kind of dreams they had. Some of those stories would stick with me. Like the one about a group of women who looked so much alike, all dressed in only black clothes. That was a sign of mourning a death in the family. The woman who was telling the story was the one who had the dream. She dreamt that her youngest brother told her that he was going far away on August twenty-third, never to come back. Coincidentally, and scarily, he never woke up on that exact day. The woman burst into tears and people were comforting her by telling her that he was in a better place and someone up there loved to have him by his side. They would whisper those words because during communism we were raised as atheists. I had no clue who that guy up there was. But it made me feel good that her brother was somewhere safe and not alone. To my understanding I thought people on those trains had a lot of pain to carry because most of the time they would go somewhere where something bad had happened. It was either that or some love story. I heard so many romances I could write a book about them.

We were going to visit my grandparents, who lived in a different city. They were from my mother's side of my family—aunts, uncles, cousins, and friends that I would be with during my winter or summer breaks. This set of friends was pretty much the same age as me and had nothing to do with my friends in the capital city of Tirana, where I lived. They were different also. They were much friendlier toward me than my regular friends. Maybe it had to do with the fact that that was how people from small towns are versus big cities. They would express their admiration freely and make me feel good and welcomed. The girls would touch my long blonde hair and hug me for no particular reason. They loved to hear me talk because, according to them, the way I spoke was different from them, without their dialect. They would die laughing when I would try to speak like them, even though later I perfected the dialect so well that you could never tell I wasn't from there. But they said, no matter how hard I tried to look like one of them, my soft skin and long hair would give me away. Girls from the country couldn't grow their hair longer because it was more practical to keep it short. This way there was less soap to buy and it kept the lice away. People in other cities were way poorer than people from the capital city.

Boys, on the other hand, would get all shy around me. They would bring me flowers or a little rabbit as a way for me to warm up to them. My closest friend there was Eni. I was terrified of the street dogs, and not because of the odd shape of their disproportional bodies or their big, square heads. I was scared of them because they were aggressive and would run to attack you at any moment. All the kids had their own ways of dealing with them: I had Eni. He was not afraid of anything.

"I wish there were a lot more street dogs around," he'd say.

"Why?" I'd ask.

"So I could help you get around, protect you, and you wouldn't be scared. Because you're a scaredy-cat, you know that."

"Don't you have something more interesting to do than pretend to protect me?" I'd tease him just to see how far he'd go.

"No. You are the most interesting thing to me."

I would not say a word; instead I'd wait for the next sweet compliment that Eni would throw at me. I must say that I liked him.

It was the first time that I would feel good having a boy around as a friend. It was something pure and innocent.

"I would fight with lions or tigers if I had to just to bring you home safely," he'd continue with his charm.

I laughed out loud and told him, "That's what you say because there are no tigers and lions around, just those leprous dogs."

Eni definitely liked anything I would do or say.

"Do you want to know how your laughter sounds?"

"How?" I'd say and look at him suspiciously.

"Like the echo on the top of the mountain: ha ha ha," he'd say, imitating me. "And your hair is the most beautiful in the world, and it smells like roses."

"How do you know how it smells?"

"I have smelled it when we play and it hits my face sometimes..." and his voice would get lower...

Toni could listen to my childhood stories for hours and I could do the same with his. He thought mine were a lot more adventurous and filled with more fun and passion...

Chapter 9

The past...

When Ben and I met, I was only seventeen years old, and he was twenty-three. We lived in the same neighborhood. He came from an elite privileged family, and his parents held important positions in the government at that time. He was a good-looking guy and ~~made~~ it was hard for him not to not catch your eye when he was around. Ben was tall with a full head of brown hair, which he never cut too short, blue eyes, and a fit body. I often saw him with pretty girls and everyone would turn their heads to see them walking down the street.

Everyone would turn One of the girls was a singer, and she was breathtakingly beautiful, not only for her physique but for her delicate gestures. She had blonde long hair parted in the middle that would move harmoniously with her body. Her light but sophisticated makeup would highlight her features even more, she was simply magnificent. She and one other girl stuck in my memory. I had seen them around with Ben a few different times. All the girls he kept around him were like them—girls from important families. They would act all humble and down-to-earth, but it was just for show. It was written on their faces that they didn't belong there. They wouldn't even look at the regular guys who were drooling all over them. Thanks to those girls, Ben had earned the nicknames Don Juan and Casanova. It was supposed to be a compliment.

He had no idea I existed, or at least that's what I thought until one rainy day. I was running to catch the local bus to school and I couldn't help but get all wet from the heavy rain. I didn't have an umbrella because the only one we had my mother had taken to work, hoping that the rain would stop by the time I had to leave. One drunk man walking in my direction offered with his alcoholic breath for me to go under his big umbrella. I ran even faster but then someone touched my arm to protect me and said firmly, "Stop there!" It was Ben.

"Come here." He then pulled me toward him under his umbrella.

"It is not necessary," I said, "my bus is coming."

"Don't lie. It just left and the next one doesn't come for another fifteen minutes. Until then, not only your curls but everything you have on will get all wet."

"And?! Why is that your problem?"

"Oh no, not at all. You're right, it's not my problem, but it for sure will be a problem for all those lucky ones who'll be forced to sit next to a wet dog for hours. Also I don't want you to get sick," he said softly since I didn't laugh at his joke.

I got a weird sense of safety from him and I didn't mind him at all.

"Let me introduce myself. I am Ben."

"Ema."

"Nice to meet you, Ema."

"Likewise," I said so formally and we both started to laugh.

He then told me how much he admired me as a girl who minds her own business and acts very appropriately when around boys. He called them predators who would go after anything that moved.

"You're a good girl, Ema."

I had no idea that I wasn't as invisible as I thought.

"From now on, no one will ever say anything or harm you ever again as long as you mention my name."

"Oh no! Thank you, but that's not necessary. I have a boyfriend to protect me if I am in need of things like that."

He got a sour look on his face.

"Aren't you too young to have a boyfriend?!"

"Not really. In two months, I'll turn eighteen. And we're just getting to know each other for now. After he finishes his studies, we'll decide and see how we feel."

"Aha, you're one of those 'modern' ones." He said it sarcastically but in a mean way, because, at that time, being seen as "modern" was dangerous because it meant aligning with Western mentality.

The bus stopped in front of us and I asked him to leave and thanked him for his gentility. He rubbed his chin with one hand and was holding on to mine with the other, like he wanted to stop me from getting on.

"Don't go to school today. You're all wet. Today is a day for having a nice conversation."

I already had one foot at the door at the bus. The driver yelled, "I'm closing the doors. Hurry up, in or out."

Ben gave him a sign to leave without me. I panicked when I was left alone with Ben at the bus station and was wondering what I had done by skipping school that day. I was mad at myself for not being firm and for taking direction from some strange boy I just met. I felt guilty but, at the same time, part of me wanted to do something unusual. Without even asking, Ben took my hand and we entered the coffee shop by the bus station. We sat and it felt good to have something to eat and some warm coffee. He was bombarding me with compliments and letting me know what a rare girl I was. Ben mentioned that I would be every guy's dream. It's a lethal combination, he said, to be pretty and smart.

"You are such a good role model for your little sister," he added. "She is lucky to have you and the fact that you guys have no father figure around, no brother. It's tough. I admire you for being you."

I would be lying if I said that I wasn't flattered by those words. It felt good to be noticed and appreciated for no reason. No one ever praised me or appreciated anything I did. I didn't even think I was doing something that needed recognition. Then he told me how he knew my boyfriend and suggested I break it off with him.

"He's not for you," he said. "He's broke as hell."

"Aren't we all?" I said in his defense.

"Not necessarily," he said in a way to let me know that he in particular wasn't broke.

It was so absurd to think that, under a communist regime, anyone could think they were somehow in better financial shape. The main theory of communism is equality. And in that country, we were equally poor, all of us. Ben somehow thought that he was above others. His cocky attitude gave him away. Maybe because equality didn't exist and the perks and privileges his family had for being loyal to the government made him think they were superior.

"Or do you want me to help get rid of him?"

"Oh no, please," I said, horrified that he would even suggest something like that.

At that moment I felt like I woke up to the realization of how senseless all this wandering around was. Chills went down my spine when I imagined how upset my mother would be if she found out about it.

"Ben, I need to go home."

"What's wrong, sweetheart?"

"I don't know how I am going to justify all this to my mother."

"Honey, you haven't committed any crime. You just broke the rules. Everyone does once in a while. I am pretty sure your mother did too."

"Ah, you clearly have no idea how my mother reacts when it comes to breaking the rules."

"What if I told you that I could fix that, would you trust me?"

"How? Tell me."

"I know your mother. Only as a neighbor—we have said hello and goodbye—but I know myself better and I can tame lions, believe me."

No one can tame my mother, but good luck, I thought to myself.

The rain had stopped. I got up and, after shaking hands with Ben, I left to go home. My mother would be there in about three hours and the fewer hours that were left, the more anxiety I felt. I was trying to make up a believable story for her but I wasn't good at lying, or maybe she was better at getting the truth out of me. The last half hour I was glued to the window, waiting for her and trying to get a glimpse of her mood. That way I would give myself some time to either change my story or not tell her at all. To my surprise, I saw her walking with Ben and entering the building. In his hands he had some flowers and a jar with peach compote. It was typically given to someone when they were sick, as something to make them feel better.

My mother seemed surprisingly happy and that instantly took away some of my anxiety.

"Are you okay, honey?" she asked nicely once I opened the door.

That rare gesture of hers caught me by surprise and I said yes. Ben came to my rescue by handing me the flowers and compote.

"Those are for you. Well deserved after what you've gone through today. I explained to your mother how a bike knocked you into the path of the oncoming bus when you were running in the rain to catch it. I told her that I stayed with you until you were back in one piece. I couldn't leave you like that and I hope that was okay with you, Miss Ema," said Ben confidently while looking at my mother, who gave him a gesture of approval.

"Oh, before I forget. We went to the neighborhood clinic just to make sure that everything was okay and they gave me that note for the school, so she can be excused," he continued and not even an eyelash of his moved. Ben looked at me with his sparkling eyes, happy to be putting on a show. As for me, I was in shock at how good of a liar he was. He then continued the conversation with my mother and gave her all kinds of compliments about her well-behaved daughters. Ben also gave all the credit to her. "It takes a mother like you to raise girls like them," he said.

Damn, he had found her Achilles' heel. He was good at that...

Chapter 10

After telling my mother that imaginary story, it seemed like Ben had been given the green light to stop by our house every once in a while and hang out with us. It didn't take long for my mother to understand that, behind that fake charm, was the other side of Ben that would come out at certain moments. He had a kind of arrogance and a sense of superiority that he could not hide even if he tried. He also had zero etiquette. Right after he'd leave, my mother had her comments about him ready.

"Those communist parents are too preoccupied with their party meetings and have no time to teach their children some manners." My mother hated that regime with a passion but would never ever express how she felt about it to anyone. It was a very dangerous thing to do. She came from a wealthy family and the government had sequestered all their assets. They did something similar to all the wealthy ones. Their excuse was that the country was destroyed after World War II and needed the money to rebuild. Also the new regime was for equality and they brainwashed people into believing that the rich made their money by using the labor of the poor.

It could have been worse. Her family could have ended up in those labor camps but, thanks to her father's smart moves, they got away from that—at least for a while. Her father had a small factory where they would produce fine wood furniture which used fine fabrics that came from trading for generations with Turkey and Greece. The trading business was interrupted immediately by the government and they took it over from then on. Under those circumstances, they were qualified to be first in line to go to the labor camps. It seemed like that was how it worked: the wealthier you were, the harder the punishment. But he not only was a successful man but also a genuine and kind human. He had put his life at risk to save wounded communist fighters by hiding them in his house. Along with the fighters a Jewish couple was hidden away from the Nazis. They were so thankful to him and never forgot who saved their lives. After the war, they wrote a letter to the president and called my grandparents heroes. I personally believe that's what saved my mother's family. The dictatorship was at the beginning phase of its installation and the president wanted to present himself as this noble person. If he threw my mother's family into camps, what would this Jewish family think of him? What if they complained to one of those international organizations for human rights? No, he didn't want that kind of attention, it was too risky. It felt like the right thing to do under special circumstances to spare the life of this particular family.

My grandfather took it well; he had no other choice but to go on with his life and try to stay outside the government's radar as much as possible. He was careful how he spoke with people and never trusted anyone. During family dinners, when some would whisper their conversations, he would repeat, almost as the refrain to a song: "There are three things you are powerless against in life—water, fire, and government." On the other hand, my grandmother didn't take it as easily as him. She fell into a depression and the moment her servants were ordered to leave, she could no longer get out of her bed. Not only because she had grown accustomed to that lifestyle and it was all she knew, but also because they were like part of the family. Meremia, for instance, had come as a baby with her own mother.

She grew up in that house; she learned the housekeeping trade and stayed to work there even after she had finished eighth grade. It was a really big deal for people with no money to go to school at that time, but my grandma had helped with that. She loved Meremia like her own child and that girl loved her even more. To Meremia, they were like family, the only one she had in fact. She would do and provide all the tasks they needed as part of her work, but she was also allowed to have conversations and was a part of every holiday, birthday, wedding, funeral—everything that a family goes through. The only time she had to totally be a servant, and she was forewarned about it, was when guests were over. But she was okay with that. She knew she was loved no matter what and that was the way things worked in life. Another thing that broke my grandmother's heart was when the police took her old wooden jewelry box. That box had been in her family for generations. As she used to say, when you wear a piece from this box, you wear a piece of your family's history. But what problem did life throw at a person that couldn't be dealt with?

As for Ben, he came from a simple farmer's family. They had been very poor due to the bad land where they were placed, and when the opportunity presented itself to them, it was a stroke of luck. After the war, they joined the Communist Party and climbed the Party ladder of career little by little. They never thought they would be such important people someday and that only grew the love they had for communism—for the party, for the president who was all for the underdogs and was not necessarily qualified. His father got a high position in the government and that was probably the main reason my mother allowed my friendship with Ben. She learned through the years how to mask her hate and be diplomatic around people. That was the survival mechanism: you adapt to your environment and surroundings.

Ben was visiting us quite often but he hadn't expressed anything to me and, as result, I had no idea what he really wanted. I didn't know what I felt for him either. He never gave me the chance to discover if I would miss him because he was always around. One late night he came over drunk and wanted to talk immediately.

"I want to be honest with you, Ema. I can't get you out of my mind. There's something about you that I have never felt before. You are a very special girl, and I would be a fool if I let you slip through my hands. But you are always so cold toward me. It's aggravating, you know?"

"What are you talking about, Ben? I am not in your hands."

"Do you know that I was about to get engaged the day I met you? I thought I had found 'The One,' but you made me change my mind. I thought my search and adventures were over, I thought I would finally have a family of my own. My parents were happier than me with my decision. I could not find anything wrong with the girl," he said as he pulled a picture from his wallet to show to me.

She was a very pretty girl, just like the other ones from his collection.

"I am happy for you but I don't know why you are trying to implicate me in all that."

"Why, why did you appear to me that day? Why did you have to ruin my peace?"

"Me?!" I raised my eyebrows, irritated by his declarations. "Please leave, you have to stop seeing me right now. I can't believe it. How could you even think I would get involved with someone else's fiancé? Who do you think I am? Leave, please…"

Ben took a clumsy step to turn around and leave but then he pulled me aggressively toward himself. I tried to fight him off but my body was too weak against his big physique. Then he gave me this kiss, and I could hardly catch my breath from its intensity. After that, he left, leaving me feeling shocked. I felt guilty without having done anything wrong. I felt bad, maybe because I thought I was responsible for shattering a relationship. Had I done anything wrong?

Chapter 11

It was getting harder and harder to get by each day in that country that was struggling economically. The deep poverty was noticeable everywhere you looked. People had that hopeless look on their faces that made them look exhausted from life. They probably felt even more tired from working all day to secure just enough money to buy some milk and bread. Finding milk and bread to buy was a problem all on its own. You had to stand in lines for hours due to the shortage of goods and most of them were given out proportionally and in accordance with how many family members you had. The government controlled how much you could eat. The stores were empty. The inventory could be done in a second just by taking a quick look around because there were no more than five basic assortments in total. It could be said that you could sense people's anger rising and that it could explode from the smallest ignition.

The group most sensitive to that miserable life was the young people. They would gather at the plazas in front of the buildings where they lived, or in those small simple coffee shops, and would talk in whispers against the government. They would drink their homemade *rakia* drink and talk about the winds of change in Eastern Europe around that time. Almost everyone was a smoker. It was one of the few indulgences they could have. They didn't care about side effects, or dying young. It made no difference to them—you're dead living like that anyway.

Everything the government did was kept secret from the public, and it caught people by surprise how some of those secrets were spilled and found their way to the mainstream. God knows how they ended up getting from the main source to people's ears. For instance, the borders of the country were guarded with heavily armed soldiers, and everyone knew that. Not just any soldiers, but ones well trained to shoot anyone who tried to escape. No one could enter or leave "The Eagle Land," that's what they called it, and if someone tried, they had to face hard consequences. For almost half a century of isolation, the slogan of government was "If an enemy has his rifle pointed at us, we have our cannons pointed at them. A total brainwashing. As a matter of fact, those cannons they were threatening to use, the most modern kind, were actually on the other side of the borders and belonged to the "enemy", who had no intention of invading us at all. It was all communist propaganda— they had no modern ammunition and an outdated army. Not everyone believed in that propaganda, and the ones who didn't were all under the impression that the world had forgotten about our existence. We wanted to be saved, not invaded by some superpower, but saved from the hell we found ourselves in. Unfortunately for us, no "enemies" seemed interested in that.

At the borders, some terrible thing had happened and no one could talk openly about it. Like the disappearance of the brother of our friend. It was a rare thing during that era for someone to disappear without a trace, because the government knew where you were at all times, unless they had something to do with it. People were talking and somehow knew that he had been executed. Supposedly his body had been cut almost in half from the hail of bullets while trying to cross the border and escape into Greece. After a week, his family was taken by an army truck to be transported to one of those infamous labor camps. No one knew where they were going, not even the members of the family who had been taken to the unknown with that terrified look on their faces. The worst thing was what happened to the uncle of one of our neighbors. They were saying that he and three other friends also tried to escape the country but didn't succeed. They had been preparing for that moment days and months in advance. They had thoroughly studied the terrain first and had checked the number of soldiers protecting that area—the spot where they could possibly enter the neighboring country where freedom was waiting for them. Either someone must have betrayed them, or it was just plain bad luck because things didn't work out as planned. They were caught only a few steps away from their destination. Those three freaking steps sealed their fate very differently and unexpectedly, but that's fate, and that's how it was meant to be. Those young boys were taken by gunpoint and directed to a hole already dug and prepared for traitors. Without any warning, they sprayed their bodies with automatic guns until they fell into their graves, and were left exposed to be eaten by animals.

One of the boys was alive and God knows why he didn't die. When it became quiet and no one was around, he tried to gather any strength he had left to pull himself out of the hole where the lifeless bodies of his friends were. He crawled over after so many other hopeless attempts tries, and the wounds he'd received made it even harder, but he fought with the mud and dirt getting in his way until he could finally get out. He had made it out of that grave but now he had to crawl to the nearest house he could see. There weren't many around, in fact there was only one. Who wanted to live so remotely anyway? For sure the people who lived in that house must have heard the gunshots. An older woman opened the door. She pulled him inside and laid him on the floor, then gave him water and went to pull out some kind of emergency kit. She tied off one of the wounds to stop the blood without asking any questions or saying anything at all. Wasn't she curious where he had come from, half-dead and covered in blood? Her reaction was like it wasn't that unusual, like that feeling when you go to the ER, thinking you're dying, but the doctor and the nurses are so calm. He must have already lost a lot of blood. Then she took some old towels and started cleaning up the floor where he lay, almost like cleaning up any evidence that might compromise her. She was not supposed to help people like that who had betrayed their country. Then she left him lying down, almost unconscious. Where did she go? In a few minutes, a squad of soldiers entered the room. All their guns were pointed at that poor boy. He looked so young—twenty-three or twenty-four maybe, no more than that. The old lady's hands were shaking and she couldn't help but give that meaningful, eye-to-eye look that said, "I'm sorry I betrayed you." But what choice did she have? She wouldn't care much about herself at that old age, but the risk she would put her children and grandchildren in if the government found out she had hid a traitor was unimaginable. She had to report him to the authorities for the sake of her family's safety. The soldiers dragged him to the grave where he had been placed before and threw him on top of his dead friends. Then, all at the same time, they shot him with a firing squad and finished him off for good.

That was only the beginning of the worst possible things that happened to families. Like losing your children wasn't enough. Those families would be declared enemies of the state and sent to some of the worst labor camps in the country where a good number of people never made it out alive. Inside of those camps, they became a number; they were nobody, nonhuman, just a number. It was hardest for females, both old and young. Living conditions were unlivable, in those slum houses with dirt instead of floors, with no electricity, and constantly trying to protect your dry piece of bread from being grabbed by rats as big as cats. And nothing could keep the guards from raping them anytime they wanted to. Whatever was going on in those infamous camps was kept secret, but somehow those secrets were circulating around and falling on people's deaf ears. They couldn't do anything about it, but they were discovering some unbearable things. One of them was about the suicide of a mother and daughter in one of those camps. They were found hanging in their room. The letter left behind for their loved ones said that it was unbearable to live with the shame and fear of getting beat up and raped in front of each other every time some coward felt like it. A terrible end was better than an endless terrible life...

During that time I was getting ready to start university in the fall. I was not speaking with Ben anymore, and my boyfriend—if I could call him that—had disappeared on me with no explanation. I didn't think about any of them. I was focused only on my school and my future goals. I knew how to fill my free time and had no problem being alone. The place where I lived was like a small world inside the rest of the city. Luckily for me there were so many young students around. We were so close with each other that it was impossible to be in a bad mood around that cheerful crowd. One night when I thought everything was falling into place and I was taking the right path in life, Ben appeared out of nowhere like mushrooms after rain. I thought he looked handsome—he hadn't shaved for two or three days and had those melancholic eyes. He gave me a hug and while he was holding me tight, whispered in my ear.

"Ema, today I don't want you to say a word. I need to talk to you. Something really bad has happened."

I knew he wasn't lying and something must have happened to him for real because his pain was very evident. I felt sorry and kind of missed him somehow, not to mention the pure honesty I felt in his words. I was all alone that day. My mother was visiting her parents in their hometown. They were sick and she went to see them as often as she could. My sister spent the weekends with my father's family. As for myself, I was content reading books in peace and quiet, or I would invite over my friends Luli and Aida. We then threw what we called our kind of parties. We felt like independent adults and would allow ourselves to drink ponc, a lighter and sweeter version of whiskey, make something simple to eat, and smoke a cigarette. Most of the times we would end up holding our ribs from laughter and causing our neighbor to bang on the wall. This was a warning for us to keep our voices down because obviously we were being way too loud.

"What's going on, Ben?" I asked while pouring him a glass of water.

He put his hands on his head, rubbed his watery eyes, and released his breath before speaking.

"The brother of my fiancé has crossed the border and is nowhere to be found. I believe he is in Greece already."

"Aren't you glad he was able to escape this hell?" I said sarcastically, mostly to let him know that I had no interest in knowing anything about their lives.

"Not really, no," he continued without noticing my irony. "To make things worse, because of him, now they are coming to take all his family to one of the most remote, harsh labor camps."

"Oh, I am really sorry to hear that," I said sincerely. "Can't your father do anything about it? He must have some kind of connections with government authorities, no?"

"No, he can't help them. Not only that, but he was warned by authorities that me and my family must separate ourselves immediately from them, otherwise we will have to face consequences as well. I'm not even allowed to say goodbye. Ah, she is so unlucky. That poor girl," he said, so saddened by the whole ordeal. "A few days ago, it was me who broke her heart. I told her that it was over between us and that we should no longer see each other. I couldn't go on like that when I'm in love with someone else."

74

"How did she react to that? And why did you do that?" I said, almost whispering.

"She was devastated. She didn't want us to give up on each other, and started calling me a hundred times, crying and wanting to talk about it. I stopped answering at some point and got so annoyed until she came to my work, which really pissed me off. I was so cold and firm to her when I told her that this was the last time she would see me. And now all this is happening."

For the first time I noticed Ben's sensitive soul hiding under his big physique. Quite often he might come off as arrogant but I also realized he had his soft spots. Since that day we somehow became good friends. My mother silently approved of this friendship. One of the main reasons must have been that a lot of arrests were taking place left and right of among families with pasts like hers. They were one of the ones spared from the government but the beast could wake up at any time and swallow them all. Secretly she wished I ended up with Ben as a security blanket for us, but on the other hand she couldn't stand him or his family. She found them rude, simpleminded, without any cultural knowledge. She even used one simple expression to describe them: "You are who you are, oregano can never grow to be a tree." She thought communists were a specific species. Most of them were ex-convicts who took advantage to climb the ladder to power. Some were naive and bought into the doctrine due to their poverty and desperation for a better life.

Chapter 12

People are divided into two categories. The ones who believe that your fate is written in the stars, and the others who believe you can write your own fate. The believers of controlling your destiny think that if you get hit by a bus while crossing the road, it's not that this was your fate, but that you didn't look around to see it coming. You ignored it, you weren't careful enough to see the danger. I had my own dilemmas regarding that theory and I wasn't sure in which category I belonged. I thought that I had done everything, or the best I could, to be able to have some control over my life. I thought I was on the right path for a better future. I had finished high school with very good grades, and as result, I got approved to study the major I wanted: journalism. The way things were going for me meant that I had been careful to look left and right for the bus—or life—coming in my direction so it wouldn't crash into me. But, no matter what, it seemed like an invisible hand was stirring my life and had total control over it. It was that invisible hand that would write my fate the way it wanted to, filled with adventures and things I didn't ask for. At times I thought the invisible fate writer had something personal against me...

My mother lost her job by getting laid off. No explanation was given to her why, but by putting two and two together, she had her own thoughts about it. She was sure they replaced her with a young devoted member of the Communist Party who had priority. After all, my mother was someone with a dark past, because that's how my mother's family was considered. She could never be a member of that party for that reason, even if she lost her mind and wanted to. My father had cut his financial support on the day I turned eighteen. The part he would continue to pay for my sister was enough to eat bread only and nothing else, as my mother would say. She looked thinner and overstressed. As if those things weren't enough for her to carry on her brittle shoulders, the cherry on top was when she got an invitation to an urgent meeting. The meeting was held by the neighborhood committee, all members of Communist Party, and was about my mother's and her daughters' appearances. Appearance meant how we presented ourselves in public, in regard to our looks. They criticized the way she dressed herself and her girls. There was no simplicity in her look, and it wasn't in accordance with the government's standards and rules of how women should appear and look. She was dressing way too chic, and chic was inappropriate in that country. It symbolized wealth; it gave her the look of a Western woman and that was against everything practiced there. The Western world was their biggest enemy.

"Look at you. Don't you think she looks like she just walked out of that catalog?" the director of the committee said, asking the others while pointing at a glamour magazine from a foreign country, which not only wasn't available to the public but was forbidden by law. My mother froze and was paralyzed from fear. Who knew what they would fabricate just to get her punished for something? They read to her how many laws she had broken just by doing something like that, and it seemed she was in deep trouble.

"This is the enemies' propaganda," he continued. "And the enemy doesn't always come with guns and swords, but with hidden agendas. What do you want to protest with your look? Do you want to trigger nostalgia for the destroyed class of the wealthy? A class that used the labor of the poor, drained their blood, and kept the money to themselves? That's what you want, right? You want people like you to rise up again. Don't get your hopes high because it is never going to happen. We destroyed your class to the ground so you will never be able to exist anymore in this country."

On the table he went through pictures of her and us girls taken by the secret service. There must have been someone following her around and trying to take as many compromising pictures as possible. Was she a target now? The director then opened the fashion magazine and made her admit the similarities between all of us and the models in those magazines. My mother was now terrified by how things were going and she knew that the story could very quickly take a turn against her. She got chills down her spine and felt her hands sweating. She knew where we could all end up if she didn't react diplomatically and quickly. She decided to play the role of being truthful and innocent. She decided to tell the truth in front of this committee, which was as ridiculously funny as it was dangerous at the same time.

"I am a single mother. I am raising my daughters without a father figure because their father decided to leave us for someone else. I try to save some money by buying fabrics, which are much cheaper, and I cut and sew them myself. I have never seen any catalog or magazine like that, and it is out of the question for me to own one. I have made some amateur cardboards with our measurements and that's how I make them. I try to make them simple because I don't have the right skills to make them any better, but if that goes against your policy, and I have broken any rules, I deeply apologize to you. I promise I won't cut any new clothes, I will just repair the old ones nicely and, you're right, the girls need to live in simplicity to be good girls."

She then looked down, humbled and humiliated, waiting to see if her Oscar-worthy performance had any effect on them. My mother told them the truth, partially at least. She knew how to sew, but it wasn't her who was sewing our clothes. She hid from the committee a small detail, the name and identity of the real seamstress, Gabriela. She was an older lady who had finished her designing school in Paris, but she wasn't allowed to work in her profession privately and she didn't want to waste her talent working in those governments factories. There they would make a few limited, almost uniform-like kind of clothes for the population. This was another kind of control they had installed—how to dress. It was like a praise to poverty. The more beat-up and poor you looked, the better your chances of being seen with sympathy by the government. Being fashionable was something they saw as an influence from the West. This country had nothing to do with the way Westerners lived their lives, and to make things worse, if someone showed them the slightest admiration, it was considered punishable by jail. Gabriela's clothes were very simple instead, but made with good taste and they fit your body like a glove.

The director looked at my mother suspiciously, and I think she got him when she mentioned repairing the old clothes instead of making new ones. He couldn't stand women who tried to deny what was obvious, but he thought that my mother was different, and was being truthful. He decided to let her off with only a warning, but if she repeated the behavior, she would face very harsh consequences...

Ben would stop by our house every day and would sometimes spend hours with us. He told everyone that I was officially his girlfriend, this way no boy could "bother" me. I wasn't able to attend university that year so I had to work any kind of job available, and there weren't many around. I settled for a small sweater-making factory. The schedule was horrific, from six in the evening until six in the morning, but the salary was better than anywhere else.

I would work at night and sleep all day. That way I would avoid seeing the students filling the buses every morning, going to school. That was hard for me to watch when I so badly wanted to do the same thing but couldn't. Their carefree attitude and confidence made me feel clumsy, and purposeless. I gathered all my strength to accept my fate and go on with my daily routine. The survival instinct won over everything. You adjust, and you have hope that things will work out somehow, even though you might not know exactly how at that moment. That was the only option I had and there was nothing more I could do besides deal with it.

The women who worked at the factory weren't as friendly as I would have liked. They were different, beat up from life and always angry and aggressive. They didn't need any reason to feel provoked and pick fights. Their fighting switch was on all the time, like a mechanism they used to protect themselves from each other. They couldn't stand me and always told me to my face that an educated girl didn't belong there, that I should be studying at a university somewhere. Ironically, I couldn't agree with that fact more but told them that I had nothing going on in that department and I was in a bad enough way to be amongst them. I wasn't a fighter; it wasn't in me. I couldn't, and if I wanted to survive there, I had to kill them with kindness. It worked, because the one they feared the most became my protector. It is said that things happen for a reason, and after some time I understood why fate had thrown me there. It was that place and those women who influenced me in such a way that I chose my profession and my future career.

During lunch it was the routine to sit around a wood stove. Everyone would put their bread on top of the stove to toast, and we'd share with each other what we brought from home. It wasn't much, since foods were limited, and there wasn't much variety, but sharing gave us a feeling of togetherness. Comments about food led to opening up about our lives. We didn't share just a meal but also our joy or problems—mostly problems, in fact. It was pitiful the way they viewed abuse from a man. It almost seemed normal to them that a husband could come home drunk and hit you because nothing was ready to eat or that they can have sex regardless if you want it or not. I don't know how I had the courage to talk to them about Stockholm syndrome, and convincing them to say no to abuse. I gave them some tips on how to do it tactfully and gain respect for themselves. They jokingly gave me the nickname "the psychologist" and they swore that some of the things I told them to do worked. I knew that not only had I gained their respect, but they genuinely liked me. I felt the same way toward them. Getting to know them deeply, I understood where their anger and frustration came from. When you know better, you do better. One day Tana's boyfriend showed up at reception asking for her. She mentioned once how afraid she was of him, and how shattered she felt every time they fought. Tana felt used when she was forced to support him financially, but she couldn't break up with him either, because he wouldn't let her. Sometimes he would manipulate her, leading her to believe that love required sacrifices, and he'd shower her with affection when she'd give him what he wanted. But once the money she gave ran out, he'd become abusive verbally and physically. That day was payday, usually the day he'd show up at her work the most. He'd take half of her salary and disappear for a while.

"Can you please tell Tana I'm here?" he asked me.

Something possessed me at that moment and, fearlessly, I got all authoritarian on him.

"No, sir. You can't see Tana any longer."

"What did you just say?!" he responded, looking at me shocked and bitter at the same time.

"Yes, you heard me. What you are doing with her is illegal, and I will have to notify the authorities on her behalf if you ever bother her again."

"And who are you to tell me that?"

"I am her new manager and I am well aware of what's going on."

I don't know how he took me seriously because I was so young to be in such a position, but what I said, and the way I said it must have convinced him enough to believe my statement. The truth is he never bothered her again. Tana was terrified of course when I confessed what had happened, but the relief she felt after getting rid of him was priceless. It took some time for her to gain her confidence back though. We never know how strong we are until we are forced to prove it to ourselves.

The way my life had turned at this time limited my ability to live my life in the same way as other friends my age. I was convinced by now that, when bad things come, you just have to open the door and let them run their course, because you're powerless against fate and destiny. Most of my friends filled their lives with entertainment after school, partying and having fun—or whatever was permitted under the circumstances—the way it was supposed to be. If you don't do stupid things when you're young, you'll have nothing to laugh at in your old age. When and if they become somebody prominent someday, those things won't matter. The most important thing was to get there. They invited me to attend those fun parties with young and carefree students from time to time. They were a bit rebellious in my eyes because they drank and danced to forbidden American music, and I admired that about them.

Ben was my official boyfriend and he would find a hundred excuses to stop me from attending. My previous boyfriend had been beaten up badly by some gangs Ben had sent with a warning to never cross my path again, not even accidentally. It was a crystal clear message sent to him and I never saw him again, but I wasn't thinking about him either. One day I snapped. I told my mother through tears and crying that this wasn't the life I chose for myself, that it had been served to me by my freaking fate—probably chosen during some kind of secret meeting either on clouds or underground, who knew where, but definitely without my affirmation. I wanted to attend school. I didn't want to spend one more minute in that factory. It was destroying me emotionally and physically at the same time— working twelve-hour night shifts for months. The only option for me to attend university was if I moved in with my dad and his wife. It was the only alternative I could consider if I wanted to change my life, and I was so desperate to do that.

I left without telling Ben. I wanted to leave him behind too. My father welcomed my decision, and he couldn't stand that I was working in a factory to begin with. He thought I was on the right path now, and he didn't know the details of how I ended up working there. My mother would have never forgiven me if I spilled the secret that we were really poor and that I had to. He was supposed to think that we lived so comfortably and content with our lives and that his presence wasn't even needed. We were supposed to give him the impression that we didn't miss him at all and that his role as father figure meant nothing in our lives. All those years we rarely met him and, as I got older, our conversations were short, scripted, and controlled by my mother about how to answer or what to say. I wonder if that had caused me to be careful and hide in my shell around people in general. I came to the conclusion that my father and I were like strangers now and didn't know each other well anymore.

Living with my mother had its own problems, but there I felt free and I was able to be in my own world. I didn't need much surveillance and, generally speaking, I wasn't doing anything to jeopardize or lose my mother's trust. Living with my father, on the other hand, was getting annoying with them monitoring everything I said or did all the time. I felt like they would provoke me purposely to do something wrong and then later would give me lectures and advice on life, the same ones that my mother had felt compelled to give. It was like they had accumulated all the advice in the world to give it to me all at once. It was like there was a competition between them over who could present themselves as a better parent to me. In my opinion, they were both poster children for parenting failures. He left us to pursue his happiness and create another family with the woman he fell in love with while he was still married and didn't have a care in the world how that changed our lives forever, or at least that's what my mother often said. As for my mother, she would leave us alone for days at a time when she was taking care of her sick parents. I heard my aunt say in front of me, "You don't have to do that, because you have your daughters to take care of. We got this." But my mother would still go there, and maybe it was her escape from us, or maybe she wanted to spend as much time with her parents as she possibly could. She knew they didn't have much time left on Earth and she trusted me to be alone with my sister. I was used to being alone since I'd done it when they got divorced and we moved out. Not only that, but I was used to taking care of my younger sister and keeping her safe. That was another secret I wasn't supposed to disclose to them. No one knew at that time— not our friends, or our neighbors—that two little girls were all alone and trying to sleep while terrified by any weird noise outside.

Living with my father was an adjustment that I had to make, and it helped that I liked the environment and people surrounding us. Taking the bus every morning with other students was a reward of its own to me. It brought my joy and my smile back. A medical student who happened to be the comedian of the group was always trying to have conversations with me on those rides. He was undeniably funny and made it hard not to be friendly back to him. He waited for me a few mornings to go to school together, until Ben appeared one day like mushrooms after rain. Ben lost it; he got so angry and wasn't even trying to hide how he felt because he unleashed all of it on that poor guy and ordered him to get away from his girlfriend.

My new friend had this shocked look on his face and didn't know how to react, but I could tell that he wasn't used to dealing with people like Ben. The embarrassment I felt at that moment was unbearable so I had to let my friend go, thinking I would gather my strength back after and would put Ben in the place he deserved to be—out of my damn life. How did he dare treat me like that?

I don't know how all that scandal fell into my father's ear, but of course, as I expected, he gave me the ultimatum not to see Ben any longer. That became a condition put upon me in order for me to live there. In case Ben continued to bother me, my father advised me to call the police immediately, that was the rule. Trying to explain to him that Ben wasn't what he thought, not dangerous in the least, was like talking to a concrete wall. He didn't want me near him for any reason. He kept saying that he was not the kind of guy I should associate with but he had no words of complaint for my new friend, the future doctor. If my father only knew that Ben was my protector, because he had no idea how hard it was to go through life every day trying to avoid all the predators who approached you the minute you walked out of your house. No male figure was around to stand up for me. My father didn't care to listen to my opinion on Ben—that meant he didn't trust me and that was hurtful. During our conversations, which turned into debates, he made it clear to me on many occasions that everything was peaceful there before I reentered his life. Those harsh words were enough to keep me up all night thinking, how on Earth would I get out of this suffocating environment?

I went to see my mother outside of our scheduled day and I didn't tell my father about it. I missed my mother and my sister. She didn't seem to be upset with me but she looked a lot thinner than the last time I saw her. Money must have been really tight for her since my salary had been cut. Another thing that really bothered her was the idea of me bonding with my stepmother. My mother saw me as a weak creature who would mold to anyone who gave me attention, at least that's what she told me once. It was a warm day in May and, on days like that, a lot of my neighbors would hang out on the stone chairs in the front yard of the building. They gathered there usually to just converse about everyday things, laugh, and have a good time.

"Ema, where have you been?" my friends asked. They seemed excited to see me and I was covered with hugs and kisses in a minute. Across the street from where I lived was a small park with wooden stools where Ben was playing shah with some friends. Someone voluntarily played the messenger and told him I had come home. He stopped the game immediately and rushed toward where I was standing. All of a sudden we were in each other's arms and he whispered how much he missed me.

"How long are you staying at your mother's place?" he asked.

"Only a few hours."

"Can I have one hour with you? Please?"

"Are you going to do something crazy otherwise?"

"Please, honey, no need to be sarcastic. I know what I did wasn't right and I apologize again, but you must know how much I hate seeing you with someone else. I'm sorry."

In my heart I knew what he did was wrong, but I also knew that he didn't know any better. Men were like that in my country, jealous and possessive. I was taught that this could be a sign of loving someone deeply.

We went for a walk by the lake. I couldn't help but pour my heart out to him. I told him everything that was bothering me while living with my father. I also told him how I felt guilty for leaving my mother alone with such a limited income, because, instead of attending university this year, I could have gone next year. Ben and his presence gave me this feeling of being safe and secure all the time and I was comfortable around him. I trusted him. I wasn't afraid of being judged or embarrassed and excessively criticized.

There were times when I thought I was being selfish and egotistical toward him. Ben was listening to me without saying a word, not approving nor disapproving. We didn't realize that time had passed by so quickly and that I'd spent a good few hours with Ben. When we returned, my mother had this upset look on her face. My father had called and he was disappointed in me for breaking the rule he'd set about Ben.

"She lied, she broke a promise, and I hope she has a good excuse when she sees me tonight," he'd told my mother.

I didn't want to go back. I could picture how it would all go—him waiting for me with my stepmother by his side, lecturing me about the wrong things I did, like a broken record. Then he'd come up with some lame form of punishment. I wasn't sure what kind it'd be because it was the first time I was in trouble. Oh, how much I wanted to yell in their faces the truth, the ugly truth, the real reason why things were going this way for me. If he had been a responsible father and looked after his family, he wouldn't have to deal with stuff like this now, but he ran off with his new lover. And now, all of a sudden, he cares?! Did he really, or was it just a pretentious thing to ease his conscience?

"Ben, I don't want to go back to my father."

"Then don't, sweetheart. I like that idea, by the way."

Excited, I ran to my mother with my decision, hoping it would make her happy too, but no. She was anxious, with that crazy look in her eyes, and ordered me to leave immediately.

"I can't have one more mouth to feed and support you through school. You know our situation, why do you want to complicate my life? It's always something. I can't ever escape from my problems," she said furiously.

I left and went outside, crying. Ben followed me.

"Oh my gosh, what kind of freaking parents are they? I feel so alone in this world. Honestly, I don't want to live with any of them.

I want to be on my own, but in this freaking country forgotten by God we don't have the luxury of options."

"Ema, I know one place where you can live."

"Where? Where is this place?" I said, wiping my tears.

"At my grandma's apartment. No one lives there, and it's been closed for a while now."

"That must be nice to have extra apartments when other people here live like sardines, two or three families in one."

"Don't stress those things. That's life, some people are lucky and some are not. I love you, Ema. I've loved you since the first day I saw you. I don't want to lose you ever, I want you to be my wife. Say yes, my love."

I got caught off guard, and the words didn't slide easily from my mouth.

"I have to think about it," I murmured. I felt comfortable around him, but being his wife?!

Ben took this as a yes...

Ben's family was very happy with the news. The wedding took place in July and was financed totally by his family. It was supposed to be the happiest day of my life, but no. I was searching for that happiness, digging into my soul, but it was nowhere to be found. It was painful and all that pain was reflected in my forced, fake smiles. I couldn't find that kind of happiness and I thought that weddings must not be for me. All I wanted was for that evening, and that wedding, to be done and over as quickly as possible.

Chapter 13

—————

The past...

The capital city we lived in wasn't like the ones in the Western world, with a million bright lights, cathedrals, art galleries, all noisy and lively. During the day our city was filled with people tired from life, walking to work or running to catch some old run-down buses. Even those limited buses probably came from China or Russia as a gift for being part of the communist brotherhood. They went so slow due to the weight or due to the fear of hurting people hanging on the doors of the overloaded buses. Some places were still using horse carriages for transportation, which was in sharp contrast to the Mercedeses-Benz used by government authorities. Stores were empty, and the young people were feeling desperate and without any future hopes. When night would swallow the whole city into its darkness, you could feel the thick emptiness it offered. It was so quiet and lifeless that only the agonizing barks of stray dogs would break the silence.

We were blessed with a little girl, Ina. Ben's enthusiasm for marriage didn't last long. He was different, and he would return home late and drunk most of the time. Ben seemed to find some kind of comfort in the hole-in-the-wall bar down the street in our neighborhood. All the drunks gathered there; all the troublemakers too. While a glass of wine turns me into a sweeter and lovelier person, it turns him into a different one, a scandalous one. Drinking to him would trigger flashback memories from things in the past, and he somehow had the need to argue about them. He had this need to win the arguments, but even when you let him win for the sake of peace, he still wasn't happy and this anger led to breaking things—on the wall, on the floor, on the table. Those episodes would fill me with anger and fear, but not only for me, for his father too, with a twist though. His father would panic when Ben would loudly complain about the government and call his father their loyal servant. His father was terrified that someone might hear those things and report them to the secret police.

"We don't want to end up in jail or camps, son," he would tell Ben in a lower, begging voice. His face showed the terror he felt inside.

One day my father-in-law wanted to have a private conversation with me. He said it was about a very serious matter and important. I looked at him with that curiosity written in my face that said, *about what?*

He said, "It's about you guys, you and your husband." I don't know why he always called him my husband and not his son when he was referring to the same person, but by now I was used to him and the way he was.

"I have arranged it with some people I know to send you guys to America."

"What do you mean, 'to America'?!"

"Yes, to work for UN," he said with a lower but firm voice. "I want you to promise me that you will work with Ben to be on his best behavior so he doesn't do something stupid. And you know what that means, to take us all down with him. I don't like how he is behaving lately, and that can jeopardize the position I hold at work. Walls have ears."

The news came to me like thunder in an open sky. At first, I couldn't believe my ears and then excitement ran through my body uncontrollably. I wanted not only to scream and jump for joy, but to tell everyone I knew. How lucky was I at this moment? Could there have been any more perfect timing than that? When things were getting worse and worse there, we were given the opportunity to live at least five years in the USA, on a continent far away. Five years far away from this useless place wasn't bad at all. After that I didn't know what could happen. My father-in-law was generously advising us how to be extremely careful with our behavior there, meaning to control every word we would exchange with anyone we came into contact with. He warned us that we'd be under surveillance from people working undercover for the government.

"Things are different there, but don't fall into the imperialism trap. Not all glitter is gold."

Similar warnings were repeated to us by the Secret Service. It was always a possibility that we'd leave the embassy and ask for political asylum there. That thought alone was very tempting, but we wouldn't do that to our families. They would be the ones to suffer the consequences.

"Everything you do represents your country. So be responsible," they said.

From our government's point of view, America was this terrible place where people suffered under a capitalist regime, where the rich used the poor and a huge disproportional gap existed between them. As for myself, I had read enough forbidden books about the true America to know the difference and not be brainwashed. Deep in my heart I had a platonic love for that faraway country, the land of freedom...

The news didn't have the same effect on Ben. He thought it was too far away. I had to have long convincing talks with him until we came to a conclusion that this could be a good thing. We knew that some kind of revolution to overthrow the government was about to happen, just like the ones happening in other Eastern European countries. The domino effect would be inevitable.

Normally parents get all teary and sad if their children have to leave for a long period of time, but not our parents. They were happy and proud of us. Not everyone had earned that kind of respect and trust from the authorities, and this was kind of a big deal. It was a privilege to be trusted by them at that level. My mother whispered in my ear:

"You are so lucky to leave behind this shithole. You're going to see the world, how excited you must be!"

A few minutes before we left for the airport, she stuck three little stones in my hand and showed me what to do with them.

"Throw them one by one behind you for good luck and to never return to this place."

I looked at her, surprised at what was coming out of her mouth. She didn't want me to come back? What was already brewing in her head?"

"I hope you stay there as long as can be, that's all," she said, trying to put an end to my suspicion.

At the airport I was feeling melancholic and had teary eyes the whole time. I was nervous also. It was my first time flying and leaving the country. Many friends and relatives were there to say goodbye.

"Don't be a stranger," "write letters to us, you guys," they would say after giving us hugs.

The travel seemed endless. It was long and tiring. I admired Ben for sleeping through the whole flight, like a baby. My thoughts kept me up and alert. I was picturing myself somewhere in one of America's neighborhoods; sweet daydreaming that was. I placed myself somewhere in a house with green grass and beautiful flowers all around. I added a dog as well, which I'd take for walks daily in the beautiful streets with tall, old trees. I pictured myself parking my car in my garage after coming back from work. What a beautiful life, just like in the movies. Dreaming doesn't cost a thing; it's free, it's beautiful...

The Revolution happened as was expected, and the communist government crumbled less than a year after we left our country. It was the last place in Europe where communism had to be destroyed by its own people. Fifty long years of brainwashing and suffering were finally over. The winds of change wrapped around that small, almost forgotten country of ours. We never went back there until after we became American citizens. For our safety, after asylum and protection were given to us, we left New York and moved to Chicago, close to some friends of ours who did the same thing. There we started a new life with a new beginning...

Chapter 14

The present...

Toni had left me tons of messages while I was sleeping. The time difference between Tirana and Chicago was seven hours. If it wasn't for that space in between, we would most likely speak to each other nonstop. For a while, we only slept a few hours at night because we'd lose track of time during our conversations. Our sleeping patterns were different also. We weren't sleeping deeply at all, but how could we be when our minds and hands were alert the whole time checking the phone for messages coming from the other side of the world. He wrote that I should wake up immediately or he would ruin my beauty sleep with a phone call in the middle of the night. He was so persistent this time, almost hoping that, telepathically, I would feel his urge.

Half asleep I checked my phone and told him to continue to write while I got ready for work and then we could talk on my way there. My routine was simple—taking a hot shower, brewing coffee in the coffeemaker in the meantime, putting on makeup, and, the last thing, choosing the right outfit for the day. Then I'd fill the coffee mug to drink it in the car and voila, I was out of the door. I turned on the car and called Toni while it was warming up for two minutes. We Skyped most of the time so we could see each other's faces as well. He appeared but not as happy as usual.

"Good morning, beautiful. How did you sleep?"

I responded with love and threw a kiss on the air his way, hoping it would somewhat fix his mood. It was obvious that something was bothering him.

"What's wrong, my love? Is it everything okay on the other side of the world, Toni?"

"Nothing is ever okay for as long as I don't have you near me, my sweetheart. I have two pieces of news for you."

"Oh, honey, shoot, what you're waiting for?"

"Which one do you want first? I have one good and one bad."

"The bad one first, of course," I said. "Leave the dessert for the end."

"I am about to lose my job. The company I work for is under hot water for money laundering. Who knew? We thought it was a legit business. Many of the accountants and engineers are being questioned to find out if they had any idea what their employers were up to. I will would probably investigated as well as the new director, but being new to that position might save me from their troubles. The employers have all been arrested. Here things work differently though. Whoever has money has the power. They can buy their freedom and blame it on some innocent underdogs 'who miscalculated numbers.' It has happened with other companies. Some of the employees rot in jail and their bosses live comfortably on some exotic islands. We live in a country of wonders. To be perfectly honest, I don't want to be around here any longer. You never know. Why risk it? Now do you want the good news?"

"Yes," I said, waiting anxiously after all those scary things Toni had just spilled to me.

"I am coming to America." he said.

"What?!! Seriously?!! Omg!!! How? When?" I said unable to hold my enthusiasm.

"Yes, my love. I have already applied for a tourist visa. Most likely I would get it with no problem because I hit all the points of requirement to qualify for one. I don't want to hear any complaining, okay?" And Toni made a funny gesture by sticking his tongue out a little.

I was in disbelief and couldn't hold some squeaky noises of excitement from coming out and repeating "love you, muahh, looooveee youuu, muahhh muahhh."

"I am starting to believe you're a mafia man, you know?"

Toni laughed.

"I believe I will be there in the beginning of July."

"Toni, that fast? July is around the corner. I can't believe that."

"Why, you don't want me there? I would never be a burden on you, my love. I know your situation. If that causes you any kind of stress I can go to Florida for a while, I have some family there. I will get situated and then we can decide how we will proceed. At least we will be on the same continent and in the same country. Does that work better for you, Ema?"

"Are you joking? No, my love. Here is perfect. I'm happy that you're coming, it just caught me by surprise. I was preparing myself to come and live there with you. Do you know how often I fantasized about that?"

"Really? You thought you could adjust to this little town of mine with not much going on, almost lifeless, just to be with me? No, my angel, you deserve better than that. You are accustomed to a different lifestyle, no need to go backwards."

"With no hesitation. Someday you will understand that this move would make it easier for everyone involved in our spiderweb. I don't care much for big cities. As for lifestyle, I can live my life the way I want to anywhere on the planet. It doesn't matter where I am but who I am with—the one who I will wake up next to every morning and go to sleep with every night. It matters who I spend my life with, someone who I love with all my heart. And that someone is you, Toni. It doesn't matter where I live as long as I am with you."

"Oh, the way you make me feel, my love. My heart and soul are filled with happiness and I have never felt like that before. Would you come here for real? To live with me?"

"With no hesitation, as I told you before. Try me. Besides the fact that here it will be much more complicated."

"Are you trying to make me lose my mind over you? Because I can hardly wait to make you mine and have you in my arms forever. To give you all the love I have, all my soul, because you deserve the world. You're the one and only for me. No matter how you put it, it is definitely easier for you if I come there. You have a lot to lose if you follow me and I have nothing to lose but only to gain being close to you."

"I'm afraid to get too happy, can you believe that? I will have you so close to me. I will feel you and smell you every moment and that alone makes my heart skip a beat. Kisses in the air now will be replaced with real ones. Oh God, that's happiness itself, can't be any better."

"What about when I come home all sweaty and tired from my construction or car wash job, who knows where fate will throw me?" he said with a voice that showed humbleness but not fear for the unknown.

"I will feel that too. I will love you the same, sweaty boy."

"Are you going to sleep over at my place sometimes? With me, like a cat behind my back, comforting me when I'm tired?"

"Only sometimes? Don't you want me all the time?"

"Ah, I'm so afraid that you will never know exactly how much I want to be with you day and night, but I can't ask you for that due to your circumstances. I will be happy with the time you would allow us to be together and I will treasure every moment."

"I am coming to live with you. Does that work?"

"Hmmm, I'll think about it."

"Hahaha, you don't have to. I have already made up my mind."

Chapter 15

That night I couldn't sleep at all. I felt that Toni would get the visa with no problems and very soon. We both agreed with the saying that if you want something with all your heart, the universe will conspire for you to have it. In this case, the energy directed toward the universe was doubled, besides the one uncontrollable, instinctive stress I was feeling wondering which direction my life would take from now on. I was happy Toni was coming to America. No matter how things turned out, whatever directions our lives would take—even if we weren't meant to be together, he'd have a lot more opportunities for a better life here. Isn't that the most important factor in life when fate meets opportunity? I was going to do everything I could to help Toni integrate as quickly as possible and build a decent life in America. After all, he would be in the Land of the Free where dreams come true, most of the time at least. I wanted nothing but the best for him. He was doing something for me that no other man would have done. How many women have had the privilege of having a man like that? Someone who would commit to such a sacrifice, to leave everything he has known all his life behind him? To leave his family and friends with the knowledge that it might take years or decades until he'd see them again? To make changes in his career and alter his lifestyle and be okay with the fact that the only person he will have in his new life, in an unknown big city, will be a woman? This is the most selfless thing you can do for someone and be totally okay with it because it's enough to know in your heart that she is worth loving. He knew all the consequences that came with that. For a while he knew he would take any kind of hard work that he'd never done before until he got on his feet. But he was optimistic and wanted to shoot himself in the foot for not learning English in advance, which would have made his life easier. He was prepared for everything he had to face and nothing seemed to bother him. Love conquers all. It was worth each and every sacrifice for the woman he loved. That woman was me. My heart would explode from joy every time those thoughts crossed my mind. The love Toni had for me was unconditional, was powerful, and he wanted nothing in return. He loved me and he committed all those sacrifices because there were no other alternatives at the moment and nothing could keep us apart.

Deep in my heart I was worried and had a guilty feeling about all of this. I knew people who stayed on expired visas, undocumented for ten years if not more, without ever seeing their loved ones. Undocumented immigrants if for any reason leave the country they weren't allowed to come back for years. I had to disclose this fact to him and make it crystal clear that he could be one of those people. But his optimistic nature would find a solution to my worries. Toni said that, no matter what, things will work out in the end just the way we want it. Another important thing I had to clarify with him was my divorce. It could take up to two years for a divorcee it to end for good, especially when assets are involved. I even told him that I might have a change of heart and not go through with it if it was emotionally hard on me and my family. I don't know why I was giving him all those suggestions. In my mind I felt like I was committing a crime for breaking up my marriage. Toni's thoughts on that were different. According to him, I was allowed to be happy and no one could hold me hostage in the name of family.

"Live your life as it comes," he'd say. "Live for the moment, stress free, and let the universe guide you in the right direction. Just follow your heart and guts, that's all. Usually they know things your brain can't accept." What I never mentioned or discussed with him was the other side of the coin. If things were to go right and exactly the way we wanted, how was Toni going to face his family? He wanted me to be his wife soon, but marriage to a woman a decade older, divorced and with a child, was taboo for people in our country. In the rare case when that would happen, the boy was seen by his friends and family as a loser who couldn't be with someone age-appropriate. And, of course, Toni would use his sense of humor regarding that too and make it seem so normal or not a problem whatsoever.

He'd say that "the moment they see your silhouette like a model, with those curves and moves when you throw your blonde hair around, when you talk with those full lips of yours, the most beautiful ones I've ever seen, when they hear your lovely voice and your sweet talk, they will understand me. My friends will envy me, because you are a miracle, please believe me.

"Stop with this nonsense, love. Don't worry yourself, you are going nowhere and you will be mine 'til death do us part. If our fate is not written on the stars, how they say it's supposed to be, I would write it myself the way we want it," he'd continue.

"Don't you think this thing is inevitable?" he'd say, asking my approval. "Isn't that why people get married? To share their life together? To share everything—the bed, the kitchen, the bathroom. To be with each other endlessly, for better or worse. Don't you want that, my beautiful Ema?"

"Have you ever thought that what we have now could evaporate, disappear? What do I have left then? What if you regret one day what we've done and leave me? That would kill me, you know. I will get older before you; how would you deal with that?" I responded.

"Have you ever thought that it could be the total opposite? You could be the one to give up on me because you might have a hundred reasons not to ruin the comfort of your established life. Out of the two of us, you are the rational one who follows logic. You're the one who can lose a lot if you choose me, Ema. As for myself, I have nothing to lose, and I'd follow my heart always."

"And what is your heart telling you?" I asked, arching my eyebrow and biting my lip, a habit I couldn't undo.

"My heart tells me that I would love you even when you're ninety years old. You are not allowed to die before that, for the simple reason that I would be an eighty-year-old cranky man. No one can love me then, and I'll have nowhere to go at that age."

"Oh, your sweet talk, I want to eat up those lips when you talk like that." And it was true, I really wanted to do that.

"Eat them all you want, they're yours."

"Mmmm, I can't wait until you're here..."

Chapter 16

Toni got his visa without any complications. He then went and purchased the airline ticket the next day, giving himself only one week to get ready and spend time with his loved ones. In the meantime, after searching extensively, I found him an apartment very close to my house. I picked purposely a place across the street from a strip mall with a produce market and little shops. When you're new to a big city, and don't know anyone, and don't have a car, all you have is your feet to depend on and they can only take you so far. The price of the rent was reasonable when compared with the small salaries immigrants make when they first arrive. And the location was excellent. It was only twenty minutes from Chicago's downtown, and ten minutes from the lake with its beautiful green parks and multimillion-dollar mansions along it. Their architecture and the beauty of the landscape left a good impression on me. I was so motivated to move to that area someday. Every time I passed by, I silently promised myself that one day one of those mansions would be mine.

I furnished Toni's apartment with some secondhand furniture that was in very good shape which I got from a store nearby. It looked so nice, tasteful and almost chic. He had to spend two weeks in a hotel though until it was ready. I don't remember much from those two weeks except for the fact that we made love like crazy and couldn't get enough of each other. I just remember the typical ambiance of cheap hotels—mahogany furniture, heavy dark curtains, and paintings with swans (I always thought those swans looked so unhappy). The memories of those days have been sculpted in my mind with the two of us drowning in our own ecstasy.

When Toni arrived, I started the divorce papers because it was the right thing to do. But I still could not leave the house anytime I wanted, otherwise I would raise suspicion and jeopardize my case. I didn't want my husband to know anything. All those years, my routine had been very predictable. Every morning I was the first one to wake up and prepare breakfast and get the house in order. After work, I was always home and usually took care of dinner, or read a book or watched a movie in my free time. Rarely I went out with my friends. As a matter of fact, I never went just to hang out with my girlfriends. I'd only go out when it was someone's birthday, wedding shower, baby shower, or a funeral—important stuff like that. They invited me every month to their girls'-night-out events, but I always found excuses not to attend. Ben wasn't a big fan of those gatherings and, if I went, he'd make sure to mention it in a negative way months later. To him those were opportunities to meet new people and fall into temptations. He viewed those things to be not meant for married people, and, according to him, married people should only go out as couples. I was aware that, little by little, I was sliding into self-isolation, but I was so tired of his nonsense fights about it that I molded and caved to his desires. So Ben, being used to having me around like an obedient puppy, would notice the sudden changes in my routine right away.

Toni was trying to be understanding. He'd ask me not to worry and only visit him when I could. I wanted to every day, many times a day, every moment if possible, but I couldn't. I went to see him the first chance I got. I would stop by his place two hours before going to work. That wasn't noticeable to Ben since he left the house at five in the morning every day. Toni and I ate breakfast together, had coffee, had nice conversations, and good laughs, always enjoying each other. Then after work, I would go and spend a couple more hours with him, but it still didn't seem to be enough, and hours felt like minutes. Toni would stop by my workplace whenever he had a chance, and my heart would jump out of my chest every time I'd see him sitting on one of the chairs in the coffee shop across from my office. One of my coworkers once asked me who that handsome boy waiting for me was. I lied for lack of a better option and told her he was my cousin from Europe, hoping she'd believe me.

Toni loved America from the day he stepped foot in it. He totally believed that he had made the decision of a lifetime coming here. Knowing that, in particular, made me feel good and relieved my guilty conscience. I felt responsible for causing those major changes in his life. He never complained, or blamed me, not even when he came home exhausted and all dusty from work. He found a job in a construction company, and every day when he came home, all white from cement, it looked like someone had thrown flour on him. Not even when his hands and face were dirty and black from fixing his old cheap car which cost less than an iPhone. He didn't want me to help him financially, and the money he had brought with him was quickly gone and consumed. He had no choice but to work long hours. I wasn't happy because that meant we spent less time together. It also became more difficult for me to arrange our meetings. By the time he got home from work, it was time for me to go home and be with my family. We couldn't see each other that often as a result. Toni would go home to those empty walls with no one waiting for him—or at least that's how he saw it—take a shower, and then open some canned food to eat. He hated eating this kind of food and mentioned often that it tasted like cat food. I didn't have the guts to joke with him about it and say, "How do you know that cat food tastes like that?" I knew it wasn't the food's fault, but the way he felt for having no one else here besides me. He'd finish the meal alone and then would take a ride in his car around my house. He'd ask me to come by the window just so he could see my face a little. He missed me so much. This was so hard for me, and I'd go by the window and swallow my tears when our eyes met. When he'd disappear at the end of the street, I would get so upset that I would grab my dog and take her for a walk just to see Toni for a minute at least. In the meantime, he would have gone around my house two or twenty-two times already in the hopes of seeing me. I'd jump in his car for five minutes. I'd kiss him without talking, with my eyes closed, to take with me some of the heavenly scent that'd keep me alive until I saw him again. I'd leave in tears.

"Why must it be like this, Ema, why? I miss you so much, my love, and I can't go on without you."

I tried to explain to him many times that it wasn't easy to get divorced from a person like Ben, because he wouldn't agree with any point of presentation made by my attorney about splitting our assets. He would drag the sessions on for the stupidest reasons and make ridiculous excuses.

"Leave him everything, Ema. Money obviously didn't buy you happiness, it has just bought you the luxurious life. Do you recognize yourself when you're at my place?"

I knew what he meant by that.

"At my place, you can't find two plates that match. Instead of luxury, there is simplicity, but you're free there, you are yourself, you are soft, you are sweet, you are lovely, you are happy. Love is life, Ema, that feeling that fills your soul in a way that no amount of money on Earth can. Life is what we have, you and me. Believe me, I consider myself lucky to experience that kind of love, even if I die without a dollar in my pocket. It is a privilege to have this happen to you in a lifetime. I am a lucky man."

"Oh, Toni, please just give me time and the world will be ours."

He had an idea that I was in very good shape financially but because he wasn't much interested in that part of my life, we never went into details. As result, he had no idea that I was a millionaire who silently lived my life surrounded by luxury. It is unheard of for millionaires to leave that wealth behind for any reason.

On one of the days he was driving around my house in the hopes of seeing me walk the dog or watering the flowers, he saw Ben entering the long driveway with his brand-new toy, an all-black Porsche Turbo 911. This was one of the latest gifts he had gotten himself. It was an addition to his already exotic collection. When I met Toni the next day, he wasn't in a good mood at all. He looked tired and his eyes had some noticeable dark circles. *Maybe he didn't sleep well last night,* I thought. I asked him nicely if he was all right or if something was bothering him.

"I know that you will never come here to live with me," he said. "I feel it. I know that you would never leave him or the lifestyle you're accustomed to. What do I have to offer you besides...ah," he sighed.

"Oh, Toni, stop. You are the one I love, and you know it. What you see is just the facade of my prison with golden bars. The fancy things I'm surrounded by haven't filled my emptiness and you know that very well. Bars are bars, even when they are made of gold. Who says you won't have those things someday too? It is in our hands to have what we want if we're focused and determined to achieve something in life."

"I won't have them. No, and I'm telling you this upfront, I would never chase money over spending enough time with my wife. I would rather fulfill her soul than her pockets. That's how it works, right?"

"What are you talking about, Toni? Don't you think you're being a bit offensive? Do you even have the smallest idea that the thing I want the most is to be with you every moment of my life?"

"And who is stopping you from doing that, Ema? Do you expect me to ask your husband for your hand? If you allow me, I'd do it without any hesitation. I will tell him the truth, face-to-face. I will tell him that I have stepped into his territory dishonestly but that I love his wife so much, in a way he never could. Allow me to tell him that 'to you she is just a part of your collections, like another Ferrari in your garage, but to me she is the world. To me she is the most valuable treasure I could ever have. Keep all the money to yourself and set my Ema free, or your Ema if you want to call her that. I don't understand why you'd want a body when I am the one who has her heart and soul.'"

"That was unnecessary, Toni," I said, irritated now and ready to leave.

I left and pulled the door hard behind me, leaving Toni upset in the middle of his living room. I regretted doing that the moment I entered my car. I tried to call him but he didn't answer. I felt my stomach turning from anxiety. After a few other phone calls, he finally picked up and his voice was shattered. It seemed like he had been crying.

"I am okay, love, and I'm sorry. I don't know why I'm so weak sometimes and unleash all of my worries on you when I promised once that I would never complicate your life no matter what. I'm sorry, my love, but it is killing me and eating me alive that you belong to someone else."

"I belong to you, my everything. You and you only, my love, with every cell and molecule. Do you think I don't want to be there right now and kiss your salty tears?"

"Come and do it. I can't take it anymore without you, Ema..."

Chapter 17

We met almost every day. Toni and I coordinated our schedules in such a way to have coffee and breakfast together before going to work. Then later, because I would finish work before him, I'd stop by his apartment. I'd either cook or order something to eat and wait until he came home to eat together. We would spend at least a couple of hours making love, only to find out with disappointment that those hours were never enough. His facial expression every time I had to leave his place would scratch my soul. Once I left, I'd be unexplainably sad. I felt terrible, because here I was, going back to my family, to my daughter, like nothing happened. This unbearable guilt was eroding me—guilt for my family, guilt for Toni, who was all alone and had no one to turn to. It was a big burden for me to carry, bringing him here for me, and I thought that it was so difficult for a person to fill every need that human nature requires. It wasn't easy for Toni to arrange plans with his construction coworkers, on weekends at least. Those were the hardest and the loneliest times, and having a beer with a friend would be a blessing, but with who? He only had two colleagues, as he would call them. One was American and a little bit of a weirdo, in his opinion, always in conflict with someone. If it wasn't his boss who'd done some injustice to him, it would be a client. He had an itch for fighting, and he didn't care much to hang out with people from work who he'd just met. The other worker was Mexican. From him, Toni had learned a couple of important things. Thanks to him, he went to get a driver's license given specifically to illegals. It was painful to see how happy Toni was to get this document that didn't have any great value, but being somewhere in the system made him somehow feel like he existed. The Mexican was married with four children, and family obligations didn't leave him much time on the weekends. And he couldn't afford the luxury of having a couple beers with his friends.

Toni started to feel the loneliness and came to the realization that the minimum wage he was making wouldn't get him anywhere or help him progress the way he wanted to. He had plenty of time, and the best way to fill those long endless weekends was to get a second job. He did find one as a pizza delivery guy at a pizzeria right next to his place. There were many young people working there who came mostly from Eastern Europe or the Middle East mostly. Almost all of them were living in America illegally because their student's visas had expired a long time ago. The good energy and the atmosphere of that place had a positive influence on Toni's well-being. He was noticeably more uplifted and didn't feel like he was the only undocumented person on Earth anymore. His new coworkers were the optimistic ones and saw the glass as half full, not half empty. It was true that, momentarily, they couldn't work in their real professions, or use the majors they had studied for, but someday they would touch and live the American dream. They were full of hopes and happy that, after all, they were living in The Promised Land. Where else can you make your dreams come true better than here? It made me really happy to see Toni in such a great mood and feeling grateful for any little progress that he made. Working at the pizzeria not only didn't tire him but it made him happy. A few days of work there with tips equaled what he made breaking his back in construction. He collected enough money to buy a newer car and get rid of the one that was about to break down at any moment. I suggested that he not keep the pizzeria's sign on top of the car, or at least that he take it down when he was done with work and entered the building.

"Why? What is the problem?" he asked, surprised.

"It's no problem, whatsoever, but I don't think your neighbors should all know where you work, or that you have a second job."

"Do you really think my neighbors care about my life? And, more importantly, do you think I care what they think of me? No, Ema. I am afraid it is all in your head. This is what you think about me. I am too poor for you. I am not acceptable by your social standards or to be seen with you. Why are you with me then, why...?"

"Toni, why do you have the tendency to misunderstand me lately? I apologize anyway. I shouldn't have said anything."

His humor changed like someone had pressed a button. He went to take a shower without inviting me to join him as he usually did. In the meantime, I had made dinner, which was ready on the table, and poured red wine in our glasses. We were eating and drinking in total silence, looking at the paintings on the walls or the designs of the tablecloth, but not in each other's eyes. Not even a comment or a compliment from him like usual. I was used to being praised constantly for my cooking and table presentation after each bite Toni took. Sometimes he would unleash orgasmic voices to convince me that the fish, or beef, or salads, and desserts were almost better than sex. That would motivate me to pour all my love and talent into cooking him some of the best dishes I knew. But not that day. That day he said absolutely nothing. He just left me with that bitter feeling of his silence deep in my soul. It was time for me to leave and go back to my family. He accompanied me to the door, looking all down and saying to me in a lower, sad voice, "Go, the jail's visitation hours are over for tonight."

I left him with a cold "good night." The fresh air and light rain felt good on my face and red cheeks...

My hands were glued to my phone, checking it constantly to see if there was any message from Toni. I wanted so badly to hear from him that he loved me so much and that we should never get to that point again. No message came that night. I tried so hard to sleep, and just couldn't. That's how dawn found me, exhausted and sleepless, searching for messages on my phone. I had no clue how I was going to function that day but I got up, got ready quickly, and drove straight to Toni's apartment. I put the key in and turned it slowly, trying to be as quiet as possible and not wake him up. He was there, behind the door, and he opened it and pulled me inside politely. He pushed me up against the door gently, and started kissing my lips, then my chin, my neck, my nose, my cheeks, my hair, while apologizing for his behavior of the night before.

"I am so sorry, my love. So sorry to transmit to you all my stress and worries. I knew how it was going to be. I know your situation, and it is not your fault. You simply belong to a different world that I'm not familiar with, but I would not want you to ever change. Please don't leave me. I cannot live without you, Ema. You are like air and oxygen to me. You are a necessity."

"Never, my love, never. I couldn't do it even if I wanted to. I'm under your spell, Toni."

"Oh, my beautiful Ema. My angel. I love you! I love you with all my heart and soul, my life..."

Chapter 18

———

Days went by and seasons replaced each other, almost faster than before, or at least that's how it felt. Since Toni came, one thing after another had changed in my life. Those long, boring days were now nonexistent. It didn't matter if we filled our hot summer days with walks by the lake or in the park, eating ice cream or dining in world-class restaurants. It made no difference even if we spent all day cuddling and making love in his apartment. One thing was for sure: Toni's presence had turned each day better than the last for me. He brought joy into my life; I felt excited, entertained, alive. I felt young, I felt beautiful and fulfilled. What we had in generous amounts was our love for each other. What we did with passion and pleasure was making love.

But the happier I felt each day, the more melancholic Toni seemed. The thought that I was playing him and he was just fulfilling the missing part of my fabulous life was eroding him like rust to metal. The truth was that, for me, he was happiness itself. I valued that more the moment I realized I couldn't have him the way I wanted to. One perfect example was holidays, and there were quite a few of them. They were killers for both of us in different ways. Holidays usually bring families together, but for Toni, whose family was far away, holidays were filled with nostalgia and sadness. The worst for him were Christmas and New Year's. Outside, the bitter winter would run its course full force while icicles created an arctic look, and the white snow covered the streets. Inside, through houses' open curtains, you'd see happy families toasting with glasses full of beverages. Toni had no one to toast his glass with. The person he loved the most was probably toasting with someone she could barely stand. That was the irony of fate—people in love who can't be together and loveless people who cohabit in misery. It seemed that the divorce was going to take longer than predicted. Unfortunately, Ben was under the impression that he deserved to keep everything, and not just what the law allowed him to keep. For him, money wasn't only something you make a living with. For him, money was power, importance, and control. I already knew that he would fight me down to my last penny...

The atmosphere at home was tense. We tolerated each other respectfully and that was a facade we kept up in front of our daughter. He was going on a trip to Texas and that came just in time for me to find some peace. Ina had planned a short trip for herself and her friends for a while now. They were going to Wisconsin for three or four days—nothing big, just a little getaway. I had a reunion to attend in Florida and was meeting my high school friends there who now lived in Canada and America. They had planned a dance party in a nice hotel and hanging out on the beach the next day. That couldn't come at a better time for me. I needed that little escape from reality at the moment. I asked Toni to come with me. After all he needed some sun too, and what better chance would we have to be with each other day and night for a few days at least? He agreed to come and drove down a day after me, since he couldn't fly without proper documentation. That way I would be able to finish the event with my friends and could wait for Toni to arrive with champagne chilling on ice and a warm seafood dinner ready to go. Another thing that he wanted me to agree with was that he was going to take care of all the expenses. He was excited that this was going to be our first vacation together and hopefully not the last. It was pointless to disagree with him about those kinds of things. For me, it was more than enough to spend all this time with him, even if I didn't leave the hotel room once.

"How is that going to work? If I pass the test of sleeping with you, are you going to be mine forever without the right to go back to where you were before?" he said and playfully stuck his tongue out.

"I don't know, love. Maybe I will be the one to fail the test, you never know."

"You passed that test a long time ago, love; that's why I'm standing here face-to-face with you. And I hope you will continue to like it because you know what? You're stuck with it," said Toni and he wrapped his arms around my waist in a way that kind of tickled me and I jumped, laughing. He kept going, harder, getting a kick out of it, while I was about to faint from laughter. He seemed to like to "torture" me like that and listen to my squeaky voices because I was unable to talk.

The condo I found was small, cozy, and pleasant. I tried to find something inexpensive so as not to hurt his budget or his feelings. It was on the first floor, with an ocean view and a huge patio. We were steps away from the sugar-white sand. The sunsets were breathtaking and colorful with shades of yellow and orange and red. The sun looked like it was dipping inside a gigantic bathtub filled with shimmery lit waves, then disappeared little by little, creating some more beautiful shades, from lilac to purple, to gray and then black. Toni loved scuba diving and he didn't take into consideration my warnings about how sharks were always present around there. I would admire him, thinking "he is not hard on the eyes" while he was sunbathing under the tropical sun, which wasn't as strong during that time of year. It was just perfect. We would stay until the sun was no longer on the horizon and then take a long shower, making love and enjoying one another. Later we would get ready while admiring our nicely bronzed, tanned skin. Hungry as we were, we'd then go eat seafood at the restaurants along the bay. Toni had the ability to make me laugh at any moment with the most spontaneous jokes, and sometimes I'd have water coming out of my nose or almost choke from it.

"When we eat, we should not make eye contact. One of these days we'll end up going to the emergency room from choking."

I wasn't as delicate or fragile as he made it seem, but it was his sharp extraordinary sense of humor that caused all the trouble. We tried to be serious and calm and act appropriate in public, but one gesture or comment from him would be enough to trigger all of our craziness. We would laugh sometimes until our ribs hurt. Toni liked to compare this place to the city by the sea where he had lived back home. Passing by fast-food restaurants or ice cream shops he'd say:

"Do you know what is missing here?"

"Stores that sell kebaba and burek," I said.

"Exactly, you read my mind. But don't you think it'd be a great place to open something like that though? There's nothing like that around, no Balkan food anywhere. Have you seen one? We are going to open one together."

Then he'd kiss me on my lips hard and excited, saying, "Why are you so special? When am I going to marry you?"

We were so happy, being together 24/7 for the first time. But what a buzzkill it was and so upsetting thinking that soon we would go back to reality and our old routine. This dream life and experience would all be behind us soon.

Chapter 19

That morning I woke up early. My hand instinctively went to grab my phone as usual. I noticed that Toni had sent me ten messages. He wrote how he pictured me sleeping, what position my legs were in, where and how my hands were, with my mouth open a little bit and how I must have already swallowed seven or so spiders. The last message said that he didn't know how he could resist coming to be next to me in my own bed. Toni mentioned that, at this point, he didn't care about the circumstances or consequences. I replied to him, asking if, by any chance, he'd had any weird dreams that had influenced him so badly to that point. He wanted for me not to go to work that day and possibly stay with him all day. He suggested we spend half of the day by the lake since it was a beautiful, sunny, warm day. The other half of the day he wanted to spend in his apartment and he would be in charge of the cooking.

"Can we have a quality day together, my love?"

"Yes, we can, sweetie, but help me find a good white lie for my boss. And it better be reasonable and believable."

"When I was back home," he said, "we had a girl in the office that would call in sick quite often. Every time she called she complained that she had a sore throat and a high fever. She knew that when you're contagious, no one wants you around coughing and spreading viruses. For that reason, she was excused. But it came to the point that she surpassed every limit and the director told her, 'I think it's time for you to take those tonsils out...'"

So that was my excuse then, sore throat and high fever. I got all excited when my boss told me to stay home and get better soon, so I had all day to spend with my love. I got ready quickly and left the house forty minutes earlier than usual. Once I was inside my car, I called Toni. We never understood how we found those endless conversations that carried on for hours and hours. I continued talking to him until I was in front of his door, and even when he opened it, we pretended we were talking to other people.

"I am sorry but I have to let you go. My wife is here."

"Ha ha ha, typical Albanian humor," I said and gave him a kiss on his lips.

"Why, what kind of humor do people, let's say from Scotland, have? Any idea?" he said and pulled me toward him. "You are my wife. You are the only woman for me. No woman ever could replace you." And he kissed me passionately without letting me go.

I wished my life wasn't so complicated. I wished I was able to be with him, live our lives together, in one place, but unfortunately I couldn't just run and leave everything behind. That would devastate my family. Was it too egotistical to hurt everyone involved just because I had found my happiness in life? The perfect solution would be to clear the air, be up-front with the truth, and start a new life with Toni. Then take whatever assets belonged to me from the divorce, and put an end to the misery of my broken marriage. All I needed was time. Was Toni going to be able to wait for me? Often I thought we were the perfect example of meeting the right person at the wrong time. Toni was trying so hard to keep the enthusiasm going, but I could sense the grim pessimism here and there in his behavior and our conversations. He would share with me the feeling of lonely nights when everyone you love is so far away. It didn't help that the person for whom you left everything behind and you wanted the most was so close to you and yet so far and you couldn't have her. You have her partially, but she is not yours. Actually, it was worse because you shared her with someone else. Those statements of his would scratch my soul and make me feel so guilty that I couldn't do more for him. I was not only suggesting but pushing him to go out more often with his new friends, whom he was really starting to like.

It was a beautiful day, with the sun shining making the greenery look even more vivid and the flowers more beautiful. Toni was driving, sometimes through the forests and parks, and sometimes along the lake. I tried to change the radio station because it wasn't on the favorite one we usually listened to.

"Ah, sorry about that," Toni apologized. "Matias's friend changed it yesterday."

I don't know why but I couldn't help asking, "Who is she?"

"She is a girl who just came to Chicago not long ago on a student visa and has started working with us. She is Moldavian and Matias's friend. Since she doesn't have a car yet, he begged me to take her home after work when our shifts are the same."

"What problem did she have with the radio?" I said, all nervous, like she had broken some ethical rule or something.

"She is a twenty-year-old girl, love, what do you expect? She is always happy and carefree, and all she does is listen to loud music and dance along to it. I wonder sometimes if she is ever tired with all that energy after working all day. Must be the young age."

"You are not old, Toni," I said and noticed that my hands were shaking.

"I'm not twenty either. Almost a decade and half older."

I don't know what button Toni pressed at that moment but I was brewing like a volcano inside, waiting to explode.

"I hope that doesn't bother you," he said calmly, while looking at me and making sure I wasn't furious about it. He must have sensed that something was obviously bothering me.

"Oh no, not at all. I just hope she gets her own car soon enough so she can leave your radio alone."

"Are you being ironic, sweetheart? Don't tell me you're a bit jealous about it." He was trying to give the conversation a humorous note.

"Oh no, not at all. I'm sorry if you got that impression."

"I never ever want to upset you, honey, and create any miscommunication over stupid little things."

"You are totally understood, Toni; no worries, honey."

"Why does that 'honey' sound so sarcastic to me?"

"I don't know why. I said it without any context."

Toni seemed hurt for the lack of trust I showed him. Wasn't I the one who always told him to go out with his friends and have a social life so he wouldn't feel as lonely as he looked? Having a social life is not just going out to drink beer and play pool with your friends but creating relationships with them. They do things for you, you do things for them. Those are the basics rules of any friendship—being there for each other.

"Ah, Ema. It's a shame that we can't be open about our relationship. Because we're hiding this from everyone, I can't take you places or to events I want to and I have to attend. It's really so unfortunate. Ah, how much I'd love to take you places. Wouldn't you?"

"And I assume you have an event coming up, right?" I said, trying not to let my voice betray me.

"Right, this weekend, Saturday night to be exact. One of my coworkers is celebrating his birthday and throwing a party somewhere downtown. Could you come? You're invited too."

"Unfortunately I can't. You go and have lots of fun, sweetheart."

I got all choked up because somehow it didn't feel right to me that he was living that typical bachelor's life that he was perfectly entitled to. He could do whatever he wanted and I wasn't his wife, after all. I was just his secret girlfriend and vice versa. Neither of us could come out openly about our romance. I had my reasons and Toni to protect. It was logical that he would have to create his own circle with his male and female friends. Even though, theoretically, I knew that was inevitable, still my mood and humor got sour.

When we arrived by the lake, we were walking in silence side by side, admiring the perfect combination of nature and architecture. Skyscrapers were separated from the big lake by the large lanes of the Lake Shore Drive. The enthusiasm around was contagious and sucked you in. It was impossible not to become part of the vibration of the giant park. There were runners with fit bodies that believed in that daily routine for longevity. But there were also people who didn't care to sweat off their calories and decided to enjoy the delicious fast food from the kiosks around. Let's not forget the yoga takers and meditators on the green grass, totally in their own world and disconnected from the rest. Toni got us two tickets to go on a water taxi ride for an hour and a half. He must have remembered when I mentioned once that this was the fastest way to learn and see the most important parts of Chicago. Once we were seated and the tour guide was about to start talking, Toni whispered in my ear, "Did you know that Lake Michigan is three times bigger than all of Albania?"

"For real?!"

"Yes."

"I didn't know that," I said softly to cover the coldness in my tone.

I felt frozen, emotionless, or the only emotion I felt was some kind of unreasonable anger toward him. How could he adjust to my situation and circumstances and wait for me without punishing me emotionally? I had to get a grip and control myself, be reasonable for Christ's sake, instead of acting like a teenaged brat.

The tour guide was talking passionately about certain buildings we were passing by and Toni seemed to be so focused and interested in Chicago's history. He would mention to me from time to time how much he loved the city we lived in and that it was where he wanted to spend his life. I was quiet and words wouldn't come out of my mouth, good or bad ones, even if I tried. Toni did notice that but left me to my own moodiness. When the boat ride came to an end, we got out of it and took the stairs, separated and without holding hands like usual. Lately he wasn't showing any affection toward me in public like he usually did. He didn't want to get me in any trouble, or that's what he said at least. We stopped to get something quick to eat, a hamburger to be exact. That gave us a subject to talk about. We threw around some lame comments about the taste or the humongous portions, which you could feed four people with. On the way back, Toni asked me if I had enjoyed my day so far.

"Of course, darling. It was a pleasure."

"Ah, you continue to be mad at me, aren't you?"

"No, I am not, okay? No." I spoke with a firm tone.

He then went all quiet and didn't say a word until we arrived at his apartment's parking lot. It was obvious that his humor had changed as well. Every feeling has energy and is contagious. He asked me if I wanted to go up to his apartment, but he was acting so cold and distant. I knew he didn't feel like having to deal with me.

"No. I better get going. I have so much to do."

"That's what I thought," he said and went to shake hands with me like he'd do with any of his guy friends. No hugs, no kisses, nothing.

I left his hand hanging in the air and told him that I wasn't Matias or any of his friends to be greeted like that, and I went to my car and drove away without even looking at him standing there like a statue and not stopping me. I got an empty feeling in my stomach and I felt that something changed irreversibly that day...

Time flies and we don't feel its speed most of the time. That day we were celebrating the two-year anniversary of Toni coming to the USA. Since, for a while now, every celebration or meeting took place at his place, this one wasn't going to be any different. The ritual was simple: a delicious cake, also delicious food from any restaurant around, some red wine chosen carefully, and plenty of love and enjoyable moments. For me at least, being with him was a necessity, and there was no going back to the way I was. I surrendered to the universe and was waiting to see where fate and destiny would take me. Since my divorce was taking forever to be finalized and over, Toni didn't want me to bring it up in our conversations any longer. He thought it would be better if we lived in the present and didn't sweat the future. Not only did he hate the way I felt after every court session, but he also felt guilty. Quite often he had asked me, if we hadn't met, would I have gotten divorced or continued to live in a loveless marriage? The answer I gave killed him. No, most likely I would not have gotten a divorce, but loneliness and depression would have shortened my life for sure. I had known and met women like that, surrounded by luxury and covered in diamonds, but if you looked straight into their souls, you'd notice the sea of emptiness they were swimming in. I asked him if his feelings toward me had changed or if he thought that it wasn't worth the sacrifice we were making and if we should pull out and go separate ways. His answer was:

"To be totally honest with you, I have thought about that too, many times in fact, but I'm powerless to take the plunge. I can't imagine not having you in my life one way or another. You run through my veins, Ema. You are my last thought when I go to sleep and the first one when I wake up in the morning. That's why, for the lack of other alternatives, let's keep seeing each other the way we are."

Toni was adjusting and integrating better and better every day into his new life in the USA. The better things were going for him, the harder it was for us to see each other due to our different schedules. We went from being used to seeing each other every day to now we barely could be together once a week. He hadn't worked at the construction company for a while now and the manager where he worked had arranged that he take care of the supply delivery for twenty-two more pizzerias. That was very satisfying and made Toni extremely happy. Someday he hoped to turn that into his own business: supplying food to restaurants. He was the most optimistic person I'd ever met and easily earned the respect of every person he came in contact with. The more I got to know him, the deeper I felt for his character and personality. I admired his qualities and so did his friends and his circle, where unfortunately I wasn't included.

I was bothered by it lately, especially when he had to attend all kinds of parties, from birthdays to bachelor parties, and engagements to weddings. I don't know where I got some sick fantasy from but it would go so far that I'd picture him meeting someone new and exciting at one those events. Maybe someone more age appropriate with no baggage, drama or divorces. I never made my worries known to him. I never asked questions either, unless he volunteered details. It appeared like this other life of his had nothing to do with our relationship, until for one reason or another we couldn't see each other and I would be a nervous wreck. I had a couple of hysterical explosions that ended up with us fighting and not talking for two weeks. That would be a boiling point for me and take a toll on what we had. There were moments when I couldn't recognize myself. I was always in a panic mode over losing him and I was convinced this was happening because I missed him so much. After we started talking again, I would turn into this pitiful creature with no backbone or pride, ready to agree to any compromise to keep someone who was slowly slipping from my hands.

Like, for example, Toni thought that, to avoid any future confrontation, we should not ask questions or give explanations about our lives during the time we weren't with each other. We should also not mention marriage and plans for the future any longer because, to him, they were the biggest prank life could play on him and talking about it caused him nothing but irritation. He once said to take it out of the equation for good. As for my divorce progress, he was no longer interested in hearing about it. According to Toni, I was free to do as I wished and what felt right for me. Toni protected my privacy rigorously, but in a moment of weakness, he'd mentioned to Marius one of his friends the real reason why he couldn't take his girlfriend out to any event. To end Marius's curiosity, he had shown him a picture of me on his phone.

"I didn't imagine her that attractive since you're hiding her all the time, but for you to go that deep with a married woman?! Why?! Why, my friend? Is there any shortage of single girls?"

"Ah, I have no explanation for that, but one thing I know for sure, I have secured a place in hell for myself," Toni told him.

I had made my decision and my focus was to finalize my divorce as soon as possible. That way things could work out just the way I wanted them to. I was going to be free as a bird and Toni would be in my life just like we once wanted. What we were going through right now was just a temporary thing and part of the process. All couples have their ups and downs and how could I blame him for anything?

Marius had received full priority lately. Toni was always doing something with him or taking him somewhere. I didn't take that well. All my whining about it would turn to aggravation and accelerate into a fight with Toni. I accused him of ignoring me and letting me down. Sometimes I would call him names when he would not pick up the phone or would hang up in the middle of my hysteria. The strange thing was that I didn't remember much of it and I hated to see Toni so hurt by it, but he was so pushed already. He came to the conclusion that we needed to stop seeing each other for some time.

He didn't put any limit on how long but he thought it was necessary and he couldn't tolerate being disrespected any longer.

"Trust is equally as important as love to me. If you don't trust me, how can we have a strong relationship together? I don't want to be your mistake or, even worse, another mistake of yours."

He asked me to return my copy of his apartment's key so I could no longer come and go anytime I felt like doing so. The whole world was crumbling at my feet. I asked him through tears to not treat me like that. I wasn't a stranger after all, but at that moment, his eyes were as cold as a frozen lake and he didn't care much for my tears, nor did he change his mind. I threw the keys down and left, slamming the door behind me...

Chapter 20

I couldn't stand not communicating with Toni. The days felt like they were forty-eight hours long instead of twenty-four. I couldn't stand not being able to focus on everyday tasks. I was torturing myself with hundreds of upsetting thoughts, instead of calmly waiting for the moment that Toni would call me back and everything would go back to the way it was. He wasn't calling though and my anxiety was unbearable. I couldn't breathe at times and I felt like something was wrong with my lungs or my heart. How could I live without him, without talking to him as I was used to? He was now my addiction. He was like a drug to me. If I wasn't on good terms with him, my balance was ruined and I couldn't function. Theoretically, I knew that a woman should never be the first one to call, especially after a fight. Many times I had advised my friends how to practice ignoring someone. In reality and when it was my turn, I couldn't practice what I preached. I lost my patience and gave him a call. He was cold but polite. He explained to me nicely why we not only should keep our distance but should start dating other people.

"We don't owe each other anything, and love is freedom" were exactly his words.

How I didn't lose my mind, I don't know. I was so crazy about him and I could never imagine myself with someone else. He was everything to me, how could he not understand that? Maybe he was the one that needed his freedom. To make things worse, the more he pulled away from me, the more I wanted him. I would overanalyze and rewind all of our crazy episodes in my mind to figure out how we ended up here. I would blame Ben for dragging the divorce process on. I would blame myself for my dilemmas of what to do and how I took a while when I knew exactly what and who I wanted. I would blame Toni for not being strong enough to fight for our love and keep his promises. I was devastated by what I was going through. I was devastated how things were turning out to be. You couldn't tell what I was going through just by looking at me. I was surprised at myself for how good I became at covering up all the chaos that went on inside my soul.

It had been exactly three weeks since I'd talked to Toni, and I'm not exaggerating by saying that I was going crazy. The person I was becoming was unrecognizable. I called Toni, I couldn't resist the temptation. He didn't pick up and that fueled my anger. Any logical person would have stopped right there and waited or given up, but my logic button didn't work, it was broken. I called him many more times and left a voice mail each time. There were in fact direct accusations and yelling about how I didn't deserve to be treated like that. I told him to man up and have the decency to respond to me. I ended with the most hurtful accusation: that he didn't come here for me but to settle in the USA. Who better than me could help him integrate into life here and teach him how things functioned from A to Z. I thought that maybe this time I'd hit a nerve and he'd respond, but no, nothing, no response. His silence was the most powerful answer.

The next morning he finally talked to me, but just to assure me that his decision was not only the right one but was necessary. He didn't give me a chance to apologize. He only asked me to give him space and leave him alone. Also he added that he was going to see someone new that weekend. First I was shocked, then I got choked up. I couldn't breathe until the anger was so powerful it turned me into a crazy creature who said every possible bad word that had been accumulating for a while now. He hung up on me and left me shaking and crying my soul out. He seemed so heartless to me at that moment. How could he pull away so calmly when I was breaking down emotionally?

I was trying to find peace and continue my normal life. I hated myself for being so stupid to fall in love. I wasn't looking for it but it had just happened. Why, why did I let it happen? Where was my mind, my maturity? Why did I think I needed more in life when I had everything possible, that most people dream of having? Maybe that was the price I was paying for being greedy, not for money, but for the desire to feel the dopamine, oxytocin, serotonin, and endorphins that we get with that one kiss. Or maybe I just found the truth—that satisfaction and happiness are not found in success and material things, but in soul fulfillment and physical touch. Then why does everyone want to be rich and chase the next best job and promotion, the next best deal or trade, just to find out that this is an endless chase and not the fulfilling kind?

What happened to that little girl that would be mesmerized by the shape of shells she'd find running around the beach, or the strangely shaped pieces of wood she'd find somewhere on the grass? Pieces of wood with holes and turns that, with my childish imagination, I thought looked like some human sculptures or like certain animals to me. I had saved them in a box and that reminded me what true happiness was. Why had I complicated my life to that extent?

Someone once said, "We live with the scars we choose." I was a "Madame Bovary" of modern times. Was it all worth it? Absolutely yes. Better to love and lose then to have never loved at all. Everything was worth it. Because the love I felt for Toni made me feel alive. Now that I didn't have him, I was a lifeless walking body. I missed him emotionally and physically and, no matter how things turned out, he was and always would be the love of my life.

Ironically all this was happening now, in the middle of the summer, when Marius bought a nice simple boat for twelve people. Marius fixed boats for a living and, of course, he'd have his own. I would picture Toni mingling with a crowd of happy half-drunk boys and girls, with music thumping and champagne bottles popping. I'd imagine him with his tanned skin and white shirt somewhere in the corner, his melancholic eyes faraway on the horizon. I was going to lose my mind, just like I'd lost sleep lately, and the only solution I found was to go away to Europe for ten days with Ina. She was constantly asking me to go see Côte d'Azur, France. The itinerary was going to be Nice for most of the days, Monte Carlo maybe for one or two, and then by the time we got back to Chicago, it would have been a month and a half without any contact with Toni. Hopefully by that time I'd have forgotten him...

It was our first time to the French Riviera and we couldn't wait to explore it from the first moment of our arrival. Hotel Negresco was beautiful, not to mention the fact that it contained so much history. It was built by a Romanian hotelier from Bucharest who came to Nice at age twenty-five with the dream and goal of building one of the most luxurious hotels that would attract all the richest from all over the world. His name was Negresco. Those hotels were like museums; and at Negresco even the chandeliers held a piece a history within them. Like the Baccarat chandelier at the Royal Lounge, with 16,309 crystals, which was ordered by Czar Nicholas the II but because of the October Revolution, it wasn't sent at the right time. During World War I, this hotel was transformed into a hospital for treating the wounded. Ironically, Negresco died poor; he lost everything because when the war ended, the number of visitors went down drastically. He was then forced to sell his hotel to a Belgian company.

Promenade des Anglais, the most famous street in Nice, was lively and filled with tourists who simply just walked or dined in the amazing restaurants around. There were two wide sidewalks and one narrow one. One was on the side where all the hotels, restaurants, and little boutiques were. One, a little smaller, was in between two car lanes. That was decorated with beautiful flowers and manicured bushes. The third one, and the widest of all, was along the beach side. There were some stairs that led down to the shores with dark gray stones. During the day it was filled with beach lovers sunbathing; during the night, with lovers who spent their romantic evenings in the beach tavernas drinking champagne, eating delicious food, and cuddling in each other's arms. Everything was so magical, from the beautiful scenery to the music played, which would soften your heart or break it into pieces. The scent of the sea was in the air, and I was intoxicated by it.

I missed Toni so much at those moments. I wanted to be with him right there and enjoy those moments, just like those lovers with eyes locked on each other and holding hands tightly. The fact that we would probably never enjoy things like that together again made me feel sad. He had no idea that, at that moment, I was so far away, on a different continent. It was a good thing, in a way, because I felt like I didn't think of him as much. The reason could be because, in this country, nothing connected me to him. In Chicago it was different because we lived so close to each other and I could feel his presence everywhere I went. We could run into each other, if not in a store, somewhere in a gas station or bank. Instinctively I would check my phone from time to time for any message from him. I was trying not to think too much though and focus on our entertaining itinerary this vacation.

During the day we'd spend a few hours by the beach, then we would walk around town, admiring the architectural miracles of France. We visited museums, old churches, and one castle by the beach many times. We liked going there all dressed up in light linen clothes with sandals and hats on. We would climb the stairs to the top of castle and, from there, mesmerized by the view, we'd enjoy the beautiful panorama of Nice. It was simply amazing and the weather was just perfect. God himself must have blessed us with the right temperature. Monte Carlo was another wonderful place to visit. The only bad thing that got us worried a little bit was that France had recently had some terrorist attacks, but they had happened in Paris. Here it seemed a little bit different, more quiet. We took rides on those red two-story open-top buses and we went around the whole town not once but twice and still couldn't get enough of its beauty. We took tons of pictures and shared them on Facebook and Instagram. We couldn't keep all the joy to ourselves, and we had to share it with others. I felt blessed and appreciative for many aspects of my life and I couldn't understand why I was willing to destroy everything that made my life so beautiful. What force was so powerful to make me lose my life balance and derail it?

Chapter 21

It was exactly four o'clock on July 14 when we got back to our hotel from Monte Carlo. On that particular day, French people celebrate Bastille Day, which is a very important national holiday for them. They celebrate the liberation from the tyranny of their king and the beginning of the revolution in 1789. The whole revolt started because King Louis the XVI was living a very extravagant life in contrast to the people of France, and that difference between them was growing deeper and deeper. It was an amazing coincidence that we got to see the parade right in front of our hotel. It couldn't have gone any better even if we had planned it. When we arrived there, the preparations had already started. We could see everything from our balcony if we wanted to, without leaving the room at all. The car traffic wasn't allowed that day between Hotel Negresco and Nice's castle. All the roads were available for visitors to walk around without cars all day and night, before and after the parade. Kids were the first ones to run freely, following their friends or hiding behind trees so their parents could find them after pretending they couldn't see where they went and were searching for them. Then there were couples in love wrapped up in their own magical world. Also part of the crowd were the music lovers of any age group that would dance to the rhythm of the live music from many bands around.

When the parade started, the enthusiastic crowd moved to the sides to create room for the show. First were the police force on motorcycles, driving slowly, precisely accompanied by clapping hands and loud cheering. After them came the army, so disciplined, one movement all together with no mistakes, holding their automatic guns or rifles against their chests with their hands, and so on and so on until it came to an end. Once the parade ended, people were again occupying the streets.

Ina and I were so tired from all that running around Monaco earlier that day. I wanted to take just a short break to recover so I could enjoy more entertainment that was waiting for us later on. There was so much adrenaline, and enthusiasm and it was so contagious that Ina didn't feel like coming inside and relaxing a little with me. She came in just to take a quick shower and left right after that. In the meantime, it got dark outside but that didn't fade the beauty of this place one bit. It was equally as beautiful at night. Ina sent me a text saying to hurry up because the fireworks were about to start and she was enjoying an "aperitif," as the French would say, in the hall outside the hotel. She had already made friends—two British girls and a woman from Atlanta joined her while waiting for the same thing. Another text came from her when she jokingly mentioned that I might not have a place to sit because the hall was already filled up. I was preoccupied by putting pictures on Facebook and conversing with my friends in Chicago. I told her not to worry because I would be fine standing since I wasn't tired any longer. The fireworks started and I could see them all miraculously from the open door of our balcony without even leaving my bed. Ina sent me another text saying that she had to move because a huge white truck had stopped in front of the hotel and was now totally blocking the view.

"If you don't see me downstairs, don't worry, I will come back quickly. I'm just going across the street to take a nice picture of the

Negresco Hotel with the festive colors of the French flag. From there I can take a better shot."

Ina had a passion for photography and I used to warn her to be careful, not like those crazy Instagram people who fell in the water, or worse, to their death from the top of a mountain while taking pictures. She probably didn't take me seriously. Young people are like that, they think they're immortal. I didn't feel like going downstairs. I was so into the conversation with my friends that I didn't care about the fireworks; after all, we had all night to be entertained if we wanted to be. I texted back to her saying exactly that and that I was watching everything from the comfort of my bed.

"No problem, *maman*." She said it in French. "I wanted to let you know that I'm so glad we came here. This is one of the nicest vacations we've had, and thank you."

"Oh, my love. You deserve it, sweetie. You deserve everything good in life. Just be careful, don't go too far."

I had a habit of finishing every sentence to her with a warning to be careful and I never knew why. Ina had always been a good child by all means. She gave my life meaning, from the day she was born until now, and made it more beautiful every day. She was mature, not only focused on achieving her goals in life, but also contributing by helping others to make the world a better place. I was so proud of her; she made me proud with what she had done at such a young age. Even though she was a really good child and had grown up, I still couldn't stop my warnings, but she didn't mind. She knew it was all out of love and care for her.

The fireworks were about to end but what I heard suddenly sounded like shotguns. The sound was different from the fireworks and it seemed so close by. Then, to make matters worse, people started screaming, frightened, and loudly.

"Oh my God, Ina!"

I ran onto the balcony and saw people running, all panicked and scared. A big white truck was driving through the boulevard at a high speed. My knees got all weak and I couldn't pull myself up to go and search for Ina. I tried to push myself by holding on to the walls and the door and dragging myself into the hallway.

"Oh, God, please have mercy. Please God, protect my daughter. Ina, where are you, love?"

I couldn't breathe and I was gasping for air. The hallway was empty. I started yelling, going toward the stairs, and at least I had the logic not to take the elevator.

"Help, somebody help me...Inaaa..."

I had no clue what had happened but I was pretty sure it was something catastrophic. A young man in his twenties came running upstairs on hallway and was banging on one door yelling:

"Open the door, open that damn door." It was in a different language but I was pretty sure that's what he was saying.

I asked him what was happening but he didn't respond. The door he was banging on opened up, and he entered it and closed it quickly. My adrenaline finally kicked in and I started running downstairs while praying to God to keep my daughter safe. I was begging him to at least have left her alive and I would take it from there. I was on the second floor when I saw Ina coming with a ghostly face, all white and yellow and unable to speak clearly.

"Mom, they're coming, Mom..."

"Oh, thank you, Lord, you're alive. Who is coming? Who are 'they'?"

"They're coming!" She screamed so hard and pulled my hand and directed me upstairs. She had the look of a person that had seen hell open up in front of her. We entered our room, locked the door, and I was trying to calm her down. She was holding me tightly and crying so hard. People from outside were filling up the hallway. I called the front desk to find out what had just happened. A boy with a broken voice, sounding like he was crying, said that the hotel is on lockdown because there had been a terrorist attack.

"Madame, close all the doors and please don't leave the room until further notice."

Ina, through tears, told me exactly what she had seen and experienced. The big white truck in front of the hotel was the one used in the terrorist attack. Ina was right there when all this happened. She saw him, and made eye contact with him because it was exactly the moment when she was crossing the road to take that picture from the other angle. She missed getting hit by the truck totally by accident. At first, she thought, *where in the world is that psycho going speeding right there with hundreds of people around?* But then she saw him keep going, taking down whatever was in front of him.

"My God, Mom, those little kids that were flying in the air left and right, and that noise of the bodies getting smashed, oh, I can't believe this is real. I want this to be a nightmare from which I will wake up at any moment now."

I was holding her tightly in my arms and gently touching her hair, kissing her forehead, and thinking at that moment that this traumatizing episode would affect her for a long time.

The first floor of the hotel had turned into a hospital for the wounded. The ones severely hurt were sent to the hospital immediately. The dead were separated on the side and covered with white sheets. Some others were trying to connect via phone with the family members they were separated from while all this happened. Everyone was clueless what was going on or how it would end up. A young American man with his fiancée from Chicago caught my attention. He was the hero that night. When people were running in horror, stumbling on top of each other to enter the hotel for safety, the American boy, Andy, took his fiancée inside and ran into the crowd to help others. He picked up three kids at a time thanks to his physique. He carried older women inside the hall and ran back again to help some more.

It was impossible to sleep that night. From the balcony, we watched the crime scene like it was part of a horror movie. First the police and then the special forces barricaded the hotel on all sides so no one could come inside that territory. A little bit further on the side you could see the lifeless bodies covered with white sheets waiting to be identified. In the morning, that view looked even more terrifying. All over the street, you could see some very noticeable blotches of dark red spots from spilled blood. Further down was the infamous white truck with a lot of bullet holes all over it. In the street were all kinds of shoes—sandals, flip-flops from kids and adults that had fallen off when they were trying to escape death. A bit further was a stroller, upside down, and a broken milk baby bottle. Close to it was a toy bear covered with blood, one bag with groceries, one long loaf of French bread, and one unbroken bottle of wine. Maybe someone had planned a nice romantic dinner that night for a special person. Was that person still alive? What about the ones they were going to dine with? And those who left their shoes behind, were they alive? If not, that meant that their spirits were hanging around, confused, wondering what was going on and why.

France declared three days of mourning after that tragedy. They were offering free psychological counseling for all tourists around the area of the attack. I don't know why we didn't take advantage of that. In fact, we refused it and thought we could get through that on our own. We all stayed quiet, sitting on the outdoor chairs of closed coffee shops or restaurants right outside of the hotel. Then we would walk on the boardwalk without breaking the silence, as did the other tourists who hadn't left yet. We nodded to each other, a gesture that meant "we're here, I'm glad you're alive as well." The more hours passed, the more we stayed in that horrible place, the more everyone wanted to leave immediately. If you stayed in the room instead, once you turned the TV on, you couldn't escape the breaking news. All the stations were talking about the same thing—the horrible terrorist attack. By now it was verified as a sure fact that the terrorist was a Tunisian who also had French citizenship. The total number of dead reached eighty-six and many more were wounded. It didn't make any sense to stay there any longer. I was trying to explain to the travel agency what was going on so we could exchange our tickets or get new ones and leave that place as soon as possible. The receptionist at the call center, probably located somewhere far away from the USA, was trying to explain to me how I was going to lose all those days with no refund for the hotel or the tickets since it was bought as a package.

"Ma'am, you're leaving voluntarily, there's no refund for that."

I told her that it really didn't matter at that point. Staying there was like being in a car accident where you were the only one to survive but were still stuck in a wrecked car. She said that it was impossible to find available tickets for that day but that once something came up, she'd notify us quickly. Every hour counted and Ina's well-being and state of mind were getting worse and worse. She couldn't take it any longer and was about to have a panic attack. We were waiting but luckily not for too long. The phone rang and the enthusiastic receptionist told us that she was able to find one ticket only, which left the next day at 9:00 p.m., with a stop in Turkey and then straight to Chicago. I told Ina to take it and go. She didn't want to leave me alone but I had to insist so she didn't lose that chance. Who knew when the next plane ticket would be available for me, but at least she would be safe in her own home and the sooner she got there, the better. I told her not to worry at all about me because I had a feeling I would leave right after her. She agreed to it, but I had an unexplainable weird feeling about it. Now the only problem to be solved was how to get her to the airport since nothing was functioning normally. The front desk receptionist made it clear to us that no one was working during those three mourning days, not even taxis.

Ah, those French people. But he was as shocked and shattered as us and tried so hard to help us as much as he could. Since it was close to impossible to find transportation, he arranged for one of his friends to give Ina a ride, but the only time it could be done was at 2:00 p.m., seven hours before her flight's departure. Since beggars can't be choosers, we took the opportunity given. My anxiety was rising and I thought I couldn't breathe at times, thinking that, after all that had happened, my daughter would be getting in a car with a stranger. Normally, I would never have agreed to this but, under those circumstances, we had no better choice and this was the only option available. I was trying to look calm in front of her and she was worried sick about me. I told her not even to think about it because, once she left, I'd be calling the travel agency every hour until they got me out of there. Ina had to agree to go on with the plan because she knew that her safety was my top priority and that I wanted her home as soon as possible.

Normally when we're on vacation, we usually complain how fast the days go by and that the vacation is never long enough, but when you want time to fly, it stops, and it feels like forever; it doesn't move. That night felt endless. I was lying down on the couch and changing TV channels one by one, trying to find something that wasn't covering the terrorist attack. Finally, I found a food channel, which I decided to watch just to keep my mind busy. We fell asleep, me on the couch and Ina beside me. By 4:30 a.m., we were up, even though it was still dark outside, but we couldn't sleep any longer. We went downstairs to the lobby to grab some water or coffee, since we no longer had any in our room, and of course, there was no room service to refill the refrigerator, but worse things had happened so that was nothing. While waiting for someone to bring them,

I nodded to a woman with two teenaged kids, a boy and a girl. They spoke English to one another and it felt like I knew her or had met her somewhere before.

"Hi, guys. Where are you from?"

"From Atlanta, you?" she said and tears were rolling down her face.

"Are you okay?" I asked and put my hand on her shoulder, trying to look her in the eyes.

"No, I am not okay," she said. "How can I be okay? I lost my seven-year-old son, I lost my husband," and she started to cry uncontrollably.

"Oh my God, I'm so sorry for your loss," I said and hugged her and held her while trying also to calm her down. We stayed like that, hugging tightly, for a minute or so. Two strangers who had never met before but fate or unfortunate events had brought us together. Ina, on the other side, was with the teenagers, hugging, crying, and comforting them. It is hard to find the right words to say to someone going through such a painful ordeal. It was heartbreaking and I felt so hopeless to not be able to do more for them.

"God takes the best ones to be close to him," I said, for lack of better words, hoping that it was somewhat comforting.

She was telling me about her life, how beautiful and almost perfect it had been until that moment when everything changed in the blink of an eye. She still couldn't believe what had happened or how.

"We were there as a family, celebrating one of our cousin's birthdays. My seven-year-old son was so happy and joyful throughout the whole vacation and he had mentioned to his father that this was the best vacation ever.

"I told him, 'son, you're only seven years old and if you continue to be as good as you have been so far, you will have plenty more wonderful vacations to come.' At the moment of that tragic occurrence, my angel was playing right in front of us, running a few steps, turning around—carefree as young kids usually are. The big white truck was coming furiously in our direction and my husband pushed me out of the way while pulling my son and shielding him with his body. But the impact was deadly—it killed him instantly and my son died a few hours later at the hospital. Oh, God, why, why didn't you save them? They had so much to live for..."

My tears were coming down and I was completely feeling what this woman was going through and also feeling so helpless. There's nothing you can do sometimes to prevent the surprises that fate has in store for us. I couldn't help but be so grateful to be standing there. We were alive and this was the most precious thing. Life can be taken away in a second without any warning. Everything else becomes secondary after that. It could be worse after all.

The lobby became filled with many journalists and cameramen from different TV stations—CNN, BBC. They were going to run a story on the American family who had lost two of their members during that tragic attack. We grabbed our bottles of water and went upstairs to our room. I couldn't get enough of hugging Ina and thanking God silently that we were alive, but I also had a heavy heart for those who had lost their lives. They came to visit this earthly paradise but ended up in heaven...

Chapter 22

It was two o'clock and Ina had to leave for the airport with people we had never met before and probably would never see again. The car was waiting behind and a little further from the hotel because, during the investigation, no car was allowed to park in front of it. This never would have happened in my world—to leave my daughter in the hands of two strangers—but, under those circumstances, I had no choice but to trust those boys with the hope that humanity hadn't lost its value. I had to give Ina my final goodbyes in front of the hotel, and the receptionist was going to take her to the black Citroen waiting for her. In the meantime, I had taken down all their information and their license plates. I didn't know if that would make any difference, if things didn't go as planned. But no, things would go right. I had to have a positive attitude about it. I tried to not only look but stay strong in front of Ina. I told her to text me the minute she arrived at the airport, which was only a ten-minute ride. When that text came from her on the phone—"Mom, I'm at the airport"—I jumped and I almost dropped the phone. I called her to make sure it was her texting and because I wanted to hear her voice.

"Don't worry, Mom. It feels very safe here, and there are many armed cops around. I am going to take a nap because I'm so sleepy and I have plenty of time. How do you feel?"

"I'm good, love, but I will definitely feel better once you arrive in Chicago."

"I can't wait, Mom. I miss everything about it right now."

At ten minutes to nine, I spoke with Ina again. She had already boarded the plane and was waiting to depart for Turkey and then Chicago. She told me that she wasn't able to sleep at all despite how tired she was. Because of what she went through, she couldn't let go of that bad feeling like something was about to go wrong. She was suspicious of everything and knew that it was just accidental and fate that she was alive. Ina couldn't wait to leave Europe. I tried to calm her down and make her feel better by promising that, once we were settled in Chicago, we would do everything possible to put all this behind us. At some point, we had to get rid of this feeling of fear that death was waiting around the corner.

"See you soon, my love. Call me as soon as you land in Turkey. Have a safe trip, doll!"

I lay down on the couch and watched BBC News. I was going to wait a few hours to hear from Ina once she already left Turkey and then go get some sleep and rest. I sent Ben a text because he had been so worried the whole time. It was a short message, just to notify him about her arrival tomorrow so he could arrange her pick-up.

The hotel was all quiet, eerily silent, and I felt like I was the only one left. Most of the tourists were European and had plenty of transportation alternatives. They could just drive to the next town, that's how small it seemed. I called reception to ask why it was so quiet and if I was really the only tourist left.

"No, madam, you're not the only tourist here, I promise you that," a young boy answered with the voice of someone who had just hit puberty.

"Can you tell me approximately how many are left here?"

"I am afraid I can't disclose this to you, madam, otherwise I would be breaking the rules of our policy, but I assure you that you're not alone."

"What kind of rules are you talking about, young boy? There are no more rules. You couldn't protect your guests, some of them lost their lives. They are gone, dead, understand? They will never go back home. This place, the French Riviera, was their last destination."

"I am really sorry for what happened, madam. Is there anything else I can help you with?"

"Hell, yes. Find me a way to leave this place—a plane ticket, a private jet arrangement, find me something like that, damn it."

"I am afraid I can't help you with th—"

I hung up on him, cutting off his words in the middle, knowing that the expression "crazy Americans" was crossing his mind.

Be strong, Ema, because you're losing your mind, I told myself.

I was feeling down psychologically and my patience was getting shorter by the minute and the fact that I was all alone made the situation even harder. I wanted to leave this hotel as soon as possible. What if I really was the only one there and no one could break the rules and admit that to me? I wanted to call someone to talk to at this moment, but who? Ben was probably with his secretary, Toni had disappeared on me, and I couldn't bother my friends at this hour. I was all alone inside a hotel in France and no one had a clue what I was going through. I couldn't help but leave a short message on Toni's voice mail: "Hey, I am in France." Out of courtesy, I thought he would respond but he did not.

My eyes were on the news and my mind was on Ina. A group of politicians and journalists were debating why these terrorist attacks were happening quite often in France and how to prevent future attacks. The opposite political party was criticizing the government for not taking the right precautions to protect the public during the parade. To my surprise, French people had a different way of coping with the tragedy. They responded with flowers—lots of flowers—and continuing to live their lives fearlessly. "Life is beautiful and terrorists will never win" was their motto.

I couldn't stop watching the news at this point, and Toni kept crossing my mind despite the fact that we didn't talk anymore. I was waiting for him to say something, something simple and comforting. My Facebook, WhatsApp, and Viber were flooded with warm wishes from people I barely knew, let alone family and friends. Toni was the only one to stay silent and it was hurtful. I was justifying his behavior with the fact that he never watched the news, and he never cared what was happening in politics, the weather, ordinary events, nothing—he could care less. Usually I was the one to inform him and keep him up to date. But if he knew something, and still decided to stay indifferent, that made me upset. I was offended, I was hurting, and that was just plain cold.

BBC News kept repeating and rewinding the act over and over again, adding some more facts about the terrorist. He was a young Tunisian who also carried a French passport, but he was unemployed and unhappy with the Western world, and that's why he was radicalized and joined ISIS. It would have been better for me mentally not to watch nonstop, but I was glued to seeing the raw emotions of random people that they captured during that tragedy. I couldn't change the channel. All of a sudden, in big letters, a warning followed by typical alarming music showed up on the screen:
"BREAKING NEWS!
A coup in Turkey!"
I was lying down on my bed but I felt like I had just been paralyzed. On the TV, one minute you'd see the streets of Istanbul filled with people screaming "Allah Akbar!" and another minute, the international airport where army forces were directed to take over the country after the coup.

"My God, why is all of this happening to us?"

In less than twenty minutes, Ina was supposed to land in that exact airport, which was now declared to be in the hands of the heavily armed rebels. They had asked all the airport employees to gather with passengers in one place. Whatever was happening there was being seen live through tweets sent to TV stations. I felt like I couldn't breathe normally and I felt my mouth watering and I just wanted to throw up. I had turned pale and wanted to scream as loud as I could to release the pain and panic I was feeling at that moment.

"Please, God, have mercy on us," I started praying with my hands toward the ceiling.

"Please, God, save my daughter and bring her home safe. Please, God, save those other people involved as well."

My poor girl, what was she going through right now? Like she hadn't been through enough already. My poor baby, she was all alone there. I was possessed with a sudden panic and felt like my soul had left my body. I could see my soul watching from above, looking down on a crazy woman crying, yelling, and screaming to no one. Then she fell down on her knees and said prayers with her hands together and eyes closed. This episode luckily didn't last too long. My soul reentered my body again. I regained some strength and was able to call Ben without taking my eyes off the news on the TV.

He was still recovering from the Nice attack we'd experienced and this was like a bomb to him. Ben ran to see everything live on CNN and his knees felt weak, seeing live what was going on. He tried to calm me down by saying that this was one of the biggest airports there, meaning that thousands of people were trapped in the same way as Ina. For sure they would find a way to protect and save them. The main thing was to try to connect with her and let her know that she should stick with the other tourists and not leave the airport on her own. I pictured her being terrified and I prayed for her to be strong. I couldn't let go of the guilt that I was feeling for putting my daughter in another dangerous situation, thinking that the faster she left Nice, the safer she would be. I was wrong, and a daughter is always safer in her mother's care. We shouldn't have separated from each other. What was I thinking? What made it worse was that she didn't want to take any money with her, thinking that she'd be in Chicago in a matter of hours and that I was the one who might need it, in case my credit cards didn't work. Ina had barely slept a few hours and I had no idea how she could stay awake or function. I tried calling her several times but got no answer. My eyes, of course, were glued to the screen, hoping that somehow she would show up on the recorded pieces being transmitted constantly. I jumped up from the couch when the thought of calling the American consulate crossed my mind. I Googled their emergency number and dialed it anxiously. It seemed like no one was picking up when, finally, a deep voice came through.

"Hello, how can I help you?"

"Hi, sir, my daughter has landed in Istanbul, Turkey, at the exact airport where the coup is taking place. I wanted to know what precautions are being taken for American citizens in this situation. I'm trying to connect with her but I haven't been able to."

"Ma'am, in a situation like that, in a coup, they're completely on their own. We can't interfere. They must use their good logic and common sense to stay out of danger."

"What are you talking about, sir? Are you telling me that no one will go and help them? How can they be left to the mercy of fate?"

I don't know why I was speaking in plural about all Americans there, but it must have been a gut feeling telling me that Ina wasn't alone.

"Ma'am, I think we're done here and I have to answer other waiting phone calls. My advice, if you connect with her, would be to stay close to the other tourists and not to leave the airport on her own."

He hung up long before I could ask my next question. I felt worse and hopeless now. I was under the impression that something could be done. Maybe not like those special forces did in the movie *Rambo,* but something, anything to rescue Americans trapped there. Reality is different from movies and it doesn't take a genius to figure that out. It came to a point when I thought I was going to lose it, but I tried to keep calm and stare at the TV screen.

"My lovely, Ina, where are you? Give me a sign that you are okay."

Nothing from her, just more intense news from the TV, more details about how all this had come to be executed in such a way. The rebels were liberals from the Turkish army, supposedly being directed by an escaped general now living in the USA, to kick Erdogan out of power. Don't they always like to blame America for something? According to them, Erdogan was pulling the country deeper and deeper into a dark era. They thought his reforms were slipping Turkey into a dictatorial regime and those "rebels" wanted the opposite. They were maybe too liberal for Turkey since they wanted their women not to cover their heads or at least have a choice. This information gave me some peace of mind but I couldn't stop replaying in my mind the horrible images I'd seen on YouTube lately. There were several recorded videos of people being beheaded like in medieval times. I got chills down my spine thinking of one American journalist who was beheaded live by those extremists despite his parents' pleas and their begging them to spare his life...

By now the news was only covering that event and was showing big crowds getting closer and closer to the airport, screaming loudly and hysterically, "Allah Akbar!" I didn't know if I was breathing or if my heart stopped at that moment because I wasn't myself anymore. Fear and panic mode was the stage I was in. All of a sudden, Erdogan himself appeared on TV and asked all his people of Istanbul to leave their homes immediately and go fight the rebels who wanted nothing more than chaos and instability. He said he was going there as well. During those announcements, the news anchor mentioned that around 200,000 people might be only meters away from entering the airport. In the meantime, rebels had taken control of some military aircraft, which were flying really low. I was confused and didn't understand which were the ones people would side with or who were "the good" ones. In the end, I didn't really care who won or who was good or bad, all I wanted was for everything to end peacefully. All my senses were sharpened to their maximum, my phone was charged 100 percent and on high volume, and I was wide awake, waiting for Ina to call me. Regardless of my worries and how sick to my stomach I was deep inside, I felt that Ina was okay and out of danger. She had a good head on her shoulders and she'd be able to make the right decision under certain circumstances. The ring tone of the Viber made me jump up from the bed. I didn't recognize the number but I picked up anyway.

"Hello, Mom, it's me. I'm okay. I don't want you to worry. I never charged my phone and have no battery, that's why I'm calling from someone else's phone."

"Oh my God! Thank God you're okay, hon. Don't separate yourself from the crowd, love, and don't leave the airport please."

"No, absolutely not, of course. I'm not leaving and I'm surrounded by thousands of people. Someone actually suggested we go get a taxi and find a hotel nearby but I disagreed. I was more terrified what might be going on outside in an unknown country than here. At least we're all tourists here and there are also plenty of Americans with me. I have to go. I'll call you later, Mom, and please do not worry. I love you..."

Erdogan had finally arrived at the airport with an enormous and tense crowd following him. But right when things were ready to accelerate toward chaos and disaster and clashing forces, the rebels dropped their weapons as they were told by Erdogan's forces. That was the only way to avoid a civil war.

Ina called again to tell me about the chaos there already. They had no water, no food, and all flights were canceled. It could take days to bring everything back to a normal routine, even though that this was the biggest airport that connected Europe and Asia with the rest of the world.

"Oh, that's terrible, Ina, but I think they will do something about it. All the world's attention is there, and they won't let people suffer, especially children."

"We hope so, Mom. I want nothing more right now than a hot shower and a good night's sleep. Those little things that we take for granted."

"Try to find a safe corner somewhere to nap a little, even for one hour or two to be able to function better, and possibly charge your phone."

It was impossible for me to fall asleep that night, but I didn't call Ina, thinking that she was going to follow through with the directions I gave her, as any mother to her daughter would. Early the next morning, right when your eyes are closed and your body is finally rested, letting that deep sweet sleep take you in, the phone rang. It was Ina. She was talking fast and rushed, trying to explain to me clearly how a Turkish girl at the airport front desk had helped her. She had gotten her a ticket to leave early the next morning for Chicago. My sleepiness went away like someone had put my head in an ice bucket. I was wide awake now and all happy from the information Ina had given me. Finally, tomorrow at 8:00 a.m. she would leave for Chicago. That was the best news ever, even though she wasn't going straight to Chicago and had to stop in New York. Ina had explained to Fatima, the Turkish girl, what had happened to her, to us, to people in Nice, and the girl had done everything she could to get Ina out of there. Like the ticket alone wasn't enough of a favor, she also arranged for her to spend the night in one of the hotels close by the airport, all complimentary with transportation back and forth included.

I told all of this to Ben. He was anxious to find out the progress and it gave him peace of mind knowing that finally his daughter was not only safe but was coming home the next day. The tension between us was gone. It's strange how, under certain circumstances, we find a perfect way to communicate something that was hard to do in the past during a normal situation. I was lying down on top of the fluffy pillows with a clean fresh scent. That was the first sign that I was finally finding some kind of normalcy and balance. We never know what is waiting to happen or how our lives can change in a matter of seconds; that's why every minute we live and breathe is precious. We never know when it will be the last moment that we will be with our loved ones; that's why we should express our love to them every chance we can get. Toni crossed my mind again and I felt sad. How was it possible not to hear from him? Not a call or a text saying, "I hope you're okay." Nothing. Only a biting silence. Could it be that he didn't know? I'd find tons of excuses for him, which allowed me to not get upset or angry with him. When you truly love someone, their mistakes don't mean a thing and don't change how you feel about them, because it's the mind that gets upset, not the heart. Love that comes from the heart is unconditional...

Chapter 23

Finally, I was back in the USA. It is admirable how human nature and survival instincts make you bounce back to reality so quickly while you're trying to move on. We started our days with our old routines and schedules, trying to leave all the bad memories behind. Life goes on and is more beautiful when you're in harmony with its frequencies. That doesn't mean you're not affected by those events that taught you about being in the wrong place at the wrong time and how near death we can be. Things change forever, like the way you look at life and your priorities. You come to an understanding that one moment you're here and the next you're not. One wrong move and you're just a spirit going in circles around your lifeless body. Don't sweat the little things. That's for sure. Because when this moment comes, does it matter how rich or successful you are? No, it doesn't matter at all. The universe will still continue to exist for thousands of years, with or without your presence on Earth. You should not wait the whole week for Saturday to come, or the whole year for summer to arrive, in order to enjoy life. Open the bottle of wine now and cheer with joy while it lasts. Only one shot is given to anyone, so don't miss that chance. Fate is flirtatious and likes to play games with you sometimes, and can be ironic at other times. That's a fact. Right at the time and moment of my life when

I was so sure who I wanted to be with, and what the most important thing was, exactly then I didn't have this person close to me. It was crystal clear to me now that there was only one who I wanted and loved with all my heart: Toni. He had disappeared on me, and that was scratching my soul. I didn't call him, even when my hands instinctively formed his number. Not even when I missed him so much and all I wanted was to hear his voice. Sometimes the desire to smell his scent, to feel his body, was so strong it almost made me faint. I wanted nothing more than to talk to him like I used to do, about everything—big things or little stupid things. He was the first person I would call when things were going right or wrong. He was the one I would cry to or laugh with until it hurt. Many times I felt the urge to call and say to him:

"Can we start fresh? Can we pretend like we didn't know each other before? Let me introduce myself. Can we talk and laugh? Can we relearn things that we already know about each other? Can we have our secrets and create inside jokes that only we know how to decode? Can we create new stories and new memories? Can we give each other a second chance?"

I didn't do it, only imagined it. Besides a place in my heart and soul, I gave Toni enough space in my mind too. He was sitting there like a permanent resident and I would have conversations with him all day long. I would create these imaginary dialogues that the real Toni never had a chance to hear. In those dialogues, we were never fighting. In fact, they were full of love, kindness, and caring, sometimes happy and sometimes kind of melancholic, depending on my mood at the moment. In reality, I had told Toni so many nasty things that I wasn't sure if he would ever forgive me or talk to me again. I had no one to blame but myself. Wasn't I the one who, when he'd passionately expressed his love to me, turned it off by mentioning a nihilist expression that he didn't like, like "the first day we meet is the day the separation starts"? Wasn't I the one to plant a seed in his mind that he deserved someone better, younger, more appropriate for him? I think I was almost doing that in a provocative way to see how he'd react, to test his limits. Would he change his mind? Would our love resist time and circumstances? Were we going to be the taboo breakers of our culture? How would his family react? But even if I was provoking him that way, I couldn't blame myself much for it. I needed his reaction, his security, which I didn't think he gave to me in the right dosage. I didn't want a man that leaves and comes back again. I wanted a man who would never leave me.

Deep in my heart I felt that it was only a matter of time and Toni would come back to me. If he ever loved me the way he pretended, it was going to be impossible for the two of us to be apart. Not only wasn't I angry or upset with him, but during those imaginary conversations, I was always on his side and justified his silence. It wasn't his fault. He got tired of waiting for me. He got tired of empty promises. Unfortunately, love is not easy nor practical. You can't control or command who you fall in love with. It does not come when you want it or when it's an appropriate time for it. Love connects you with someone that you didn't predict and you might face unbelievable obstacles. In the end, none of this matters because those obstacles and difficulties are exactly what determine how true that love is. Of course, it is not practical at all, but true love is the best thing someone can experience in life...

Chapter 24

When I returned to work, I was greeted with love and kindness from my coworkers and, for a few days straight, I had to tell the story of what happened to us over and over again. Then the story went away, closed, like nothing had ever happened, until a well-known TV station wanted to do a special report on us. The producer easily convinced me that our story should be made known to the public and, if nothing else, would at least cause people to be more careful and alert while traveling. Lately those incidents were occurring quite often in Europe. Ina agreed as well and felt that it was her duty as a humanitarian to participate. The producer and the journalist we worked with were very pleased and thankful because of the high ratings the special received. People are surprisingly drawn to dramas and tragedies. They show more interest in traumatizing, dramatic events than happy ones. Could it be that when we think that the world is filled with bad people and drama and trauma, it makes us appreciate our lives more?

There is an old Hebrew saying about it: "Place all your problems on the table, and when you see other people's problems dropped there, you will take yours and run."

The station ran it several times that day. Toni was at work as usual that day and, right when he was about to leave, out of the corner of his eye, he caught a familiar face on the screen. He was shocked because he had no idea that we had escaped death on the French Riviera. He sent me a text:

"I am shocked you're still alive."

Someone might have thought that was a cruel joke but it was one of our things to be sarcastically funny with each other. I responded in the same tone.

"The devil cannot burn in hell, you know that."

"Believe me, I was terrified when I saw the news, Ema, but your name wasn't mentioned. At this point i knew you were okay. I thought my prayers went to waste. I must say they were times I wished you vanished, but here you are, and this is supposed to be funny."

I burst into laughter and said, "You might consider a religion change because your God whom you're praying to is not answering your prayers any longer."

Toni wasn't very religious; he always said he believed in the universe.

"Welcome back, anyway," he said, trying not to act overly friendly with me. He wished me good night and stopped texting right after.

I felt frustrated. Here I was, with all this adrenaline rushing through me, with my eyes wide open and no sleep coming whatsoever, but Toni had decided to just tease me with that short text exchange. I wanted to talk to him, I wanted to see him, oh how much I wanted to meet up with him. Just the thought of being with him got me all teared up and I fell into melancholy...

"Good morning!" was the expression that made me jump for joy the moment I looked at my phone the next morning. It was just two simple words but the real meaning of it got me all excited. I knew it meant "I want to talk to you as soon as possible."

It was early and everyone was around so I couldn't call him. Toni always hated it when I had to wait for everyone to leave so I would be able to talk to him. He felt like an obedient dog, waiting for the owner to order him around. He had given himself many nicknames and he'd made them sound funny, but I could sense the sharp cutting sarcasm underneath those jokes. It bothered me that he felt this way, and I tried so many times to let him know that how he sees it from his point of view and how I felt were totally different things. He didn't understand that he was always with me, regardless if I was alone or in a room full of people. He never left my mind, heart, and soul. Toni was always with me, like he had spread roots all over me. That was the way it was; I couldn't change it even if I wanted to. And, of course, I left the house twenty-five minutes earlier than usual.

"Hey, what's up?" I spoke with a lower, sexy voice because I wanted to show Toni that I wasn't mad at him, that I had no questions, and didn't want to argue. My voice signaled only love.

"Not much," he said. "You're the adventurer, who went to the other side of the world to escape from me, but almost didn't make it back."

"Well, unfortunately for you, I did come back."

"You can go again. There are plenty of rivieras around the world. Every time your ego is bruised, pack and try to escape for a change."

"Haha, if it isn't the ironic man of the century. As the saying goes, if you have to choose between love and adventure, always pick adventure. Love leaves you, adventure is yours forever.

"I am starving. Besides I learned a new egg omelet recipe and I want to show it to you. Have breakfast with me, Ema."

I pretended I had to look at my schedule in order to fit that breakfast into it, but I arrived at his apartment parking lot in record time. I took off that day. The moments I spent with Toni were magical and that was the world I had created where I felt fulfilled and the whole experience made me happy for once in my life. If I had problems, stress, or worries, they would disappear the moment I entered his place. Someone said that the best kind of sex is the one you have after an argument or a fight. They didn't lie. Toni doesn't simply have sex, he makes love. His lovemaking starts at the moment he lays his emerald green eyes with thick dark lashes on you. When he doesn't interrupt that stare, you feel like your heart will stop or skip a beat at any moment. Then he takes your hands kindly and kisses them softly—the back, the palm, the fingers, all the way to the tips. After that, his fingers are tightly wound with yours and he pulls you closer and starts kissing you slowly while your body is shivering and goose bumps are covering your body uncontrollably. By the time he has finished with your neck and shoulders and has reached your lips, he puts one of his hands under your hair and whispers to you how much he wants you at this moment, how much he missed you. Gently he touches your lips with his thick ones and stays like that for a little while, smelling or sniffing you like he is breathless by it already. I think his scent is what put the spell on me, because after smelling it and feeling his kisses, I'd lose control and ask him to do things to me, unimaginable things. But that has an effect on him, the kind that causes his eyes to change and his irises to get bigger, like when animals hunt their prey. He becomes less gentle, and is more strong and powerful and has you under his control, under his desirable body that makes you turn into something wild. You feel like you are only half human and half something else that you have never met before. He is physically very strong and can turn you onto your back with one move, and with his voice deep but lower and making some light noises from excitement, he will get inside you and make you almost scream rhythmically, lower to higher notes from the ecstasy of the moment. When it gets bad, he turns you around in front of him and you beg him to be inside you, which he does. This time it's not gentle at all; you moan and scream but he puts his hand over your mouth and smiles, seeming to enjoy that you are turned on like that. It gets even better because you bite his hand and his eyes get darker when your legs meet on his back while his hands are under your butt cheeks. All you know is that when he gets to that point, releasing all his passion and sexuality like a river of secretions coming out of you and him, you moan, you cry, you sweat, you shake, you're dead but more alive than you've ever been.

I was crazy about him, for the way he made love to me. As for Toni, he'd say every time, "I don't want to ever stop making love to you."

"I feel you with every cell of my body, Ema. I never felt and I never will feel the same way about a woman if I don't have you in my life."

I had told him my biggest fear: losing each other exactly when I have fixed the circumstances because we met at the wrong time in our lives. My fear was that he would get tired of waiting and being alone and at the moment I'd be ready, he'd be in someone else's arms. Before he didn't like to even joke about it. One time he got all teared up, saying:

"Ah, you will never understand what I feel for you. I hope that this is not just an entertainment of the moment for you while, for me, it is like the air that I breathe."

Things had changed. He did not try to prove his love to me anymore...

I had to tell and retell the whole France story to my friends and family tens of times, but to Toni I just gave a short summary. I was more interested what he had been up to while I was gone and I asked him directly if he did anything spectacular or crazy.

"I wouldn't call it spectacular, but you would call it crazy. I met a girl and I've gone out with her twice already."

I choked up and got angry. Maybe it wasn't right but I had an urge to rip off his white T-shirt that fit his body so well and made him so attractive. I also wanted to turn the whole table upside down, to break a glass or something on the wall, but I calmed myself down and of course did nothing but stand there.

"Who is she, and where did you meet her to click that fast?"

"That fast?! These things don't need much time, they simply happen. She is Armenian. I thought we had things in common like similar cultures and our upbringing. I thought she sounded interesting and she paints like you. I found some similarities between you and her, but then I realized that it wasn't right. It was actually wrong to look for a woman when you have someone else in mind; that's why I couldn't continue with the third date."

"And?! What happened?"

"Nothing. I am under some spell or you have done some black magic to me since I look for you in every woman."

"I will kill you, Toni, I swear I will kill you," I said and started to hit him on his chest while he pulled me and started to kiss me.

"Kill me, Ema. That might be better. This is not the life I imagined. You left me alone. How long can I wait?"

"Not much longer, my love. Could you be patient a little bit longer? Don't give up on me, on us, on what we had, still have. You must love someone so much in order for them to feel the way we do for each other. Don't be a fool, thinking that one day this might be over and you'd live happily ever after with someone new, because you won't. Most likely you'll find out it was just a trick to escape the reality."

"Is this psychological pressure?"

"No, it's the truth. Love is energy, it never disappears. You can bury it alive somewhere, but you can't kill it."

"I don't know what to do, Ema. Part of me wants to be with you all my life and part of me wants to go as far away from you as possible. I feel guilty. I have done wrong and ruined someone's family. Someone who's done nothing wrong to me."

"Those things have no logic, my love. I also never thought I would experience a forbidden love, but now that I have found you, I don't want to ever lose you. I can't even imagine my life without you in it.

Do you remember what you once told me when I was struggling with my dilemma? 'All's fair in love and war.'"

If I went the whole year without seeing Toni, right at the moment I met him again, things would go back as they were and time would have no meaning or purpose. We couldn't spend the evenings or nights together but when we spent time together, we enjoyed every moment. I'd glow from happiness, and him being in the greatest mood made everything run perfectly smooth and joyful. The only thing that changed was that Toni didn't want to talk about plans for the future and that was bothering me a little. Sometimes his phone rang and he'd move a little further away to talk, and sometimes he'd get random text messages that he ignored, but I was trying to act indifferent about it. It gave me peace to not think about those things. He started to spend his weekends with his friends—mostly Marius—so it was unnecessary for me to find excuses to leave my family on Sundays. He didn't introduce me to his friends. At times I thought maybe he was trying to protect my privacy or was embarrassed to tell them he was involved with a married woman. People judge those kinds of things. But every bit of suspicion would evaporate when we'd spend those steamy loving hours in his apartment. We had furnished it tastefully and we didn't even want to go anywhere else most of the time. Sometimes when we were in those moments, when I was leaning against his body with my head on his chest, I'd ask questions just the way I wanted.

"What if I never leave your place, what do you think would happen?"

He'd kiss me, hold my face by my chin, look me in the eyes and say, while tucking my hair behind my ear:

"No, you won't stay, because you don't feel that kind of love to do such a thing. I fulfill whatever is missing in your life but not everything. Your ego is bigger than your love, so stop playing with me, my love."

His statements made me sad at times. I wanted to explain to him the whole process but, instead, I'd go silent and change the subject. Instead of living in the moment and thinking how lucky I was to be loved that way, in the back of my mind, like a hammer hitting me, were the thoughts that, someday, there would be no more love. I had this fear that, someday, he would leave me; then what? How would I explain this to my family and friends? Would they judge me? Even if they didn't, for sure it would cross their mind, the saying that "karma does not forget." I needed more time to make sure this was a real thing. I couldn't risk my life like that. In the meantime, we could continue loving each other. For how much longer though? That was the question. He once promised to stay with me like this all his life, if that was the only option, but would he stay true to his promise? How could I even expect something like that? It wasn't fair, of course. Toni often jokingly mentioned that I was holding his heart hostage. And, truthfully, I wasn't going to give it back to him. That was a sure thing. I couldn't live without him. Actually, I had tried. I really tried to picture my life without him but I felt like I had swallowed acid. So, no, never, not me at least, I wasn't going to be the one to leave him.

One day he asked me something weird. It was a beautiful fall day and we were looking out the window at the yellow leaves falling on the ground. He said not to say "I love you" to each other any longer. He had his hands wrapped around me from behind when he spoke firmly like that. I thought he was a bit sad, thinking that winter was around the corner, or maybe fall reminded him there comes a day when everything that once bloomed dies. Usually I'd shower him with many loving words, expressing what and how I felt for him, so how could I change that now? According to him, the "love" word was a sacred one, and it should only be used for people who meant something deep to you. Someone who was like your other half, someone who you'd do anything just to be with and who, otherwise, you couldn't live without. After all, how could I survive without hearing it from him? That was like a punishment; it wasn't fair at all. The thought that he might feel I don't deserve those words any longer was going to corrode me like rust corrodes metal. It wasn't going to be that hard, because there comes a moment when you get tired and stop giving love if it's not reciprocated.

One thing was for sure: without love, I was an aggravated and hysterical creature. I missed the old Toni. I missed what we had. It is said that hope dies last. My hope must have had seven souls because not only did it not die, it made me fall into some of those ugly compromises with myself. If I wasn't as crazy as I was for him, Toni would have simply been a memory from the past, long ago. But, as I fell, gravity was taking me down the hill rapidly and I didn't know how to stop it. It was the opposite for Toni. He had gained his strength and had changed from someone who was willing to accommodate and work around my schedule to someone who was selfish, indifferent, and almost cold. If I would try to find the time to see him and it wasn't always easy to do so, he'd get so upset and pretend to be busy for the whole week. I tried many times to be spontaneous, but that didn't work either, because he always had something supposedly scheduled with freaking Marius. The more Toni would pull away from me, the more I wanted the divorce with Ben to happen as soon as possible. Ben, on the other hand, was making it harder for me purposefully and I didn't understand why. We were separated already; I didn't belong to him and he didn't belong to me. It was over, we were just living under the same roof, that's all. We lost each other a long time ago, or it would be safe to say that we got together because of the circumstances at that time. We didn't hate each other, we'd just run out of love...

One day I decided that I truly wanted to spend the whole day with Toni, to reconnect, to bring back the times we had before. I wanted to feel him and have him to myself for hours and hours so I could bring my peace back into my soul. I got all dressed up nicely and decided to surprise him with my visit. As I was about to knock on his door, he was about to leave. His face lightened up and got all smiley, but when I asked if he was going somewhere, he said that yes, he was going to have lunch with a friend. And he had to be there in fifteen minutes to be exact, so there was no chance for my plan to go through at this point. At first, I went all quiet but then my aggravation started to come out in the form of fighting. He took it as me being controlling, which he didn't like.

"Toni, since when don't I take any priority in your life anymore?"

"Since the day I realized I'm not yours and you're not mine, Ema."

I was furious and about to lose it while I complained how badly he was treating me lately.

"No, Ema. It's you that doesn't like to be rejected about anything possible because you think the world revolves around you all the time. The moment your capricious requirements are not met, you get angry and mad at me while you're confused and don't know what you want in life."

"How dare you talk to me like that, Toni? My life is in agony but not because I'm confused or don't know what I want. It is because, look at what is happening? The one I love is refusing to be with me, to give love to me, to be with me when I need him the most. I'm a woman. I crave love and attention. What you're doing to me lately is torture. Why don't you tell me how you feel about me? Do you still have feelings for me? Tell me the truth, Toni. Set me free at least. Don't keep me hostage if you don't love me."

"I am keeping you hostage?! Are you kidding me? No, darling, no. I have simply rearranged my priorities. Ema, darling, I am not your toy that you play with when you feel like it and, if not, get thrown in the corner until you feel like playing with it again. I came from the other side of the world for you, to be with you, to have you as my wife someday, as someone I want to spend the rest of my life with.

But look where we are? You with your husband still and I'm all alone with no one around. All alone and on the leash like a dog, waiting for the owner to come home. Waiting for you so, hopefully, you find some time to fit me into your busy schedule and your fabulous life. It's about time that I start to live my life, don't you think? I have waited enough, I believe."

"Do you still love me, Toni, because you knew that all what you mentioned existed prior to coming here. Are you sure those are not excuses?"

"I don't know, Ema. I don't know who I love anymore. I love the Ema who promised me the world but instead just played with my heart. I love the Ema who was sweet and had a kind smile, the one that, once her eyes met mine, gave me that warm feeling that went straight into my soul. I'm afraid I can't love the cynical or selfish Ema."

"My gosh, Toni, why don't you say it's over? When a man loves a woman, she can do no wrong."

"Ah, Ema, please, don't start with this now. I have to leave, I'm already late."

"Can you please call and cancel on him? Say something came up. You can't leave me like this. I need to talk to you. I think it is necessary."

"No, I can't call and cancel on him. Life is not all white lies and manipulation all the time."

"Toni, can't you see that you make me feel really bad when you treat me like that? I'm all happy to see you and be with you, but once you give that kind of treatment, I suddenly get in such a miserable mood."

"If you feel mistreated, then make decisions about your life instead of telling me what to do."

"What is that supposed to mean? Come on, you never man up and tell me to leave your place when I've stayed there for hours and hours. You see what a position and chaotic situation I put myself in. You see me wrapped up in flames and just quietly watch me burn."

"Because I loved you, damn it. I did. I loved you more than I loved myself, knowing that you were with someone else, but I was too weak to let you go because I have that fear deep in my heart that I will never love anyone else the way I loved you. I didn't ask you to stay or go because that decision belongs to you and should come from your heart. What if you had regrets if I pushed you, how do you think would make me feel? I did not want to influence you a bit because I could not have lived with the guilt that I made you do something you weren't sure of."

Toni wasn't just pointing things out but screaming in tears, which left me frozen in shock like a statue, trying to absorb the difficult words he said. The most painful part was that he spoke in the past tense: "I loved you," meaning that he doesn't feel the same now. I got a sick feeling in my stomach, like a ball filled with these bad things was trying to find its way out, and it was anger. I had to let it out.

After I left, I called Toni while driving my car in an unknown direction. I was crying my lungs out and yelling at him for not being strong enough to get what he wanted in life. I told him that he was weak, otherwise he would fight to have someone he loves or loved. I didn't hesitate to tell him that maybe he didn't deserve my love or maybe he wasn't good enough for me. He'd never seen me like that, sending off ten offenses in a minute, but I must have touched a nerve because he blocked me on social media and phone without warning. I now turned into an unleashed beast. I'd call him from a private number and he'd answer, but what he'd say wasn't what I wanted to hear. Toni told me that what I had for him wasn't love, because he thought love was to let someone go free. Love is peace. He had no idea that I could turn the world upside down for him. It was obvious that communication between us was lost and we weren't on the same page any longer.

The rest of the day we argued I left him alone. The next day I left him three voice mails as that was the only option now available for me. Finally, he didn't resist; he answered and we started talking again. He didn't apologize as I was expecting and, as for me, I had the ability to go back to him with a fresh start, like nothing had happened before. All it would take was just to hear his voice and everything felt normal again. That voice, combined with his calmness and logical way of presenting things, would make me forget that we were fighting the day before. That was the biggest difference between us. If Toni got his feelings hurt, it was very hard for him to go back to normal. He would hide them inside but they would come out sooner or later. While I would enjoy our joyful moments freely, he'd be careful not to say things that might turn me into "that Ema" he didn't like. I thought this was becoming our routine; we'd fight for certain things and then get back together more passionately. We were like a bad but necessary thing for each other. We didn't lose our sense of humor, at least, and that would make it easier to connect. He would call me a paranoid maniac and I'd call him a sadistic sociopath who gets pleasure by torturing me. Usually we'd end up in bed making crazy love. One thing didn't seem to change at all—the desire we had for each other. We didn't meet as often as before, due to our schedules, and I took it as avoidance from him. I felt like I was losing him and didn't know how to change that. Whose fault is it if the leaf falls from the tree? Is it the wind who shakes it or the tree for not holding it tightly and never letting it go? Or maybe it's the leaf itself who got tired of trying to be strong. I must have read that somewhere...

The universe, fate, and destiny had their own agenda and that could be what was pulling Toni away from me. I couldn't believe my ears when he mentioned that he had seen a psychic. That's when I knew how desperate he seemed about his future. He must have been struggling emotionally to do such a thing. Even though he got all embarrassed about that because smart and educated people don't do stuff like that. But his mind got stuck on what the psychic had said to him: something like, you've got to get out of the existing relationship in order to enter a new one. The new one is your destiny and together you will have three boys. I knew that he liked to believe this was going to happen and was going to try to build his life around that: looking for the one, his destiny. I think that's how psychics work. They use their intuition to spot what is bothering you. Usually the main issue people have in common is relationship or money problems. Those can take a toll on our well-being. Then they create a story, something you want to believe. In this case, a brunette that you will meet either at work or through friends. Duh... of course, those are the most common places where you meet people. Until, one day, you start creating scenarios in your mind of those things magically happening with new people that you meet. And you're convinced that this is fate or destiny, but it is not. The truth is we create our own destiny; what comes as a result is exactly what we have created, not what it was meant to be.

I had a flat tire and Toni was the person I called for help. We tried to act like friends, using casual small talk, but our gestures and our harmony would tell otherwise. We had this undeniably strong chemistry that was hard to control. Later on, when we got back together again, he told me that while he was pretending to just be friends, he was fighting the desire to make love right on the spot. The tension was even higher now that we were supposed to be friends only and give no explanations about our separate private lives. Toni even opened a Facebook page but we weren't friends there. For some reason, everything he posted he made public, like he wanted me to see all his activities. Some of the pictures were taken going out or spending time at the beach, showing off his figure but in a very casual, innocent way. Many young, beautiful girls commented generously about his assets. I don't know why

I was so bothered by it; I had no clue who they were. I decided to play the same game. Every time I would go out to have fun, I'd make sure Toni knew all about it. I started going to the gym and, during our friendly conversations, I mentioned my good-looking Croatian personal trainer. I liked the effect it had on Toni, my whining about hard-core, bone-breaking exercises this trainer would make me perform. It seemed like he was trying to hide some kind of jealousy, and when I'd ask him how his life was going, he'd respond:

"Can't get any better. Great! Every day a new girl," he'd say and he'd wait for my reaction.

I knew he was doing this to get on my nerves, so I'd crack a joke or something and he'd laugh hard. Sometimes, after those moments, we would end up in his apartment to make love because the tension between us was too irresistible. The more appropriate word was "sex," as a matter of fact, because how we did things now was different than the lovemaking before. It was almost like a pornographic episode: hard-core sex without many kisses but which led up to exhaustion. My knees were weak when we were done but my soul was emptied out. I'd prefer to stay close with him and feel his heartbeat, smell his skin, admire his features, listen to him talk, but Toni didn't want that anymore. He thought it wasn't a good idea to continue with that kind of relationship. Why was I silently agreeing to this? Was he sliding out of my life or was I losing myself? I didn't know how to name our relationship now, but Toni called it "friends with benefits."

To my surprise, our friendship was getting deeper and deeper. We were at the point where we knew or shared our deepest secrets with each other, things we wouldn't dare share with anyone else. We would get each other's opinion on almost everything, from finances to dealing with work, friends, or family problems. We even knew each other's bank accounts, and we trusted each other without any doubts. Everything was going well for Toni—he was now that businessman from Europe with that adorable accent that made him even more attractive. He continued to keep his private life mysterious to me and that was eating me alive, I couldn't deny it. I was living my life, looking happy and full of adventures on the surface. Mysteriousness causes curiosity. One evening, after I lied to my family, I decided to spend the whole night at Toni's place after he insisted I do that. He had prepared a romantic dinner, serving a good vintage wine he'd saved for special occasions. When he opened the door, he looked at me in a way that made my hair go up on every part on my body, then he hugged me and held me tight.

"You are so beautiful and magical, and I can't fight any longer the attraction I have for you."

I was stunned. My eyebrows went up instinctively and my lips were half open from the effect of those words because, while they weren't the best I had heard from him, they were the best I'd heard in a while. I wanted to make sure this was happening for real, and he must have felt that because he pulled me gently and started kissing every inch of my face in such a way that I thought I'd faint in his arms. He couldn't get enough of kissing and smelling me, closing his eyes, whispering his affection to me, as he continued to kiss every inch of my body now. Toni's ecstasy was now the same as when we first made love to each other. We made love—a crazy kind. We didn't want it to end. We wanted it again and again until we slept on each other's bodies, feeling every beat, smelling every scent of our sweet, sweet love. We didn't want that night to end, or those moments, or that love.

"I want to be inside you endlessly. I have missed you so much, Ema."

"I've missed you more, my angel. I love you so much."

He didn't say I love you, but "let's not hurt each other anymore."

Chapter 25

We started seeing each other often again. I was totally happy now. I caught myself singing for no reason at home while cooking or doing stuff around the house. I was noticeably enthusiastic at work, and when I was with my friends. I didn't want to admit that Toni held the keys to my happiness somewhere in his pockets. I asked him to possibly do something about those girls on Facebook who would comment on everything he did or didn't do. He deleted them without hesitation, but he mentioned that it made him happy that I kind lost sleep over them. What made our closeness even more special was that Toni's sister had won the green card lottery on her first try. She was a math teacher and her husband was a doctor. They had a three-year-old son and lived in Italy for nine years, but they couldn't work on their professions there. It is hard for any immigrant in Europe to do that in general. When we used to talk about them, I suggested they try the lottery, knowing that if they won, a different life full of opportunities would be ahead of them here. Not only would they be better off here, but how awesome for Toni to have someone from his family close by? I had never seen a family as tight as theirs, with so much love and caring for one another. I wasn't used to those kinds of harmonious families. He was willing to sacrifice anything and spend his last penny to help them succeed with their plans. His kindness and positive energy had been contagious and made me feel the same way. I felt like someone from my family was coming; I got excited and wanted to see them.

We spent a few days buying extra furniture here and there to complete his apartment. We added a small bed, and some toys for his nephew. This would be the first time Toni would see him; so far he'd only talked to him on Viber or Skype. The day before their arrival, we filled the kitchen shelves and the refrigerator with all kinds of foods, chocolates, and snacks to make their coming more welcoming and comfortable. We celebrate things with food and drinks after all. I didn't want to put Toni on the spot by asking how he'd introduce me to them, but I couldn't help asking where and how we'd meet during the months they'd be staying at his place. He was always able to read me without even talking.

"We will find a way, honey. First, I will introduce you as my good friend and, this way, you can be with us often. I have told my brother-in-law about you without going into detail, but I have only met him twice since he married my sister because he lived in Italy. To be honest, I have no idea how they would react about our relationship and I don't know how open-minded they are."

"Toni, you haven't committed a murder, honey; you simply fell in love with a woman outside of our cultural standards." I felt like he was trying to convince himself more that this was the right thing to do.

"Ha, ha, no, my love. But I didn't realize that one day we would have to face the reality with facts and the truth. Don't worry, everything will go smoothly."

"I'm not worried, sweetheart. I would never make you choose between me and your family because I will understand any outcome. I know how important they are to you. What you do for them, and your kindness, is touching and makes me love you even more. Being presented as your friend is just fine and, after time, I hope they understand our love regardless of the circumstances."

It was obvious how much I loved him and vice versa, so why would they be against such a thing? It seemed like we were closer again and our relationship was warming up as it had been in the beginning, but we were still careful with words, thinking that we were in a fragile stage and that things could break at any moment. I couldn't help but think that they would influence him in such a way and tactfully pull him away from me. Another factor working against us was the lack of a place to hang out in private. Half joking, Toni had mentioned how he'd miss those days walking naked around the house at any time of the day or night. But when he saw my sad facial expression, he assured me that where there's a will, there is always a way...

When his sister and her family finally landed in Chicago, he texted me: "they are coming out, I'll talk to you later."

He didn't ask me to be present and I wasn't upset about it. I was happy for him. I pictured them hugging each other and I knew how much love there was in those hugs. Then later they would take the luggage and talk nonstop on the way to his apartment. During their dinner and while drinking wine, they'd catch up on their life stories. Most likely they'd bring up memories and laugh, as usually happens on those kinds of occasions. They would bring up childhood stories about family members, some of whom aren't around any longer. They would cry, or laugh, and who knows what else. I felt sorry I wasn't there with them, for part of it. I would die to listen to the things Toni did when he was a child, or to anything as a matter of fact. But I had to suck it up; he hadn't seen them for so long and it wasn't fair for me to complain about it. After all, they would be here all their lives so there would be the right time to do those things...

The first few days, we barely exchanged a few sentences since Toni was with them all day. Two weeks passed by and we couldn't see each other, besides having coffee a couple of times somewhere in the neighborhood. I missed him so much and had some kind of anxiety or a bad feeling about something unexplainable. I still kept all my feelings inside and didn't say anything to Toni. He seemed tired but very happy—the happiest I'd seen him in a long time. His nephew was already attached to Toni and wouldn't leave his side. As for his sister and her husband, Chicago was like love at first sight for them. They liked it the moment they stepped their feet in it. Lucky for them, their university diplomas could be converted here and all they had to do was take some tests on a couple of subjects.

"It is a totally different game when you're legal here," Toni said, "unlike me, illegal. Keli, my brother-in-law, started working directly at one hospital. Eliza has to take care of her son for a little while but I'm pretty sure she can work on her profession as well here."

I felt not only sorry but somewhat responsible for Toni, even though I had no fault in his legal documents.

"I took Keli to work with me at the pizza place for a couple days a week, so he could really taste the real life of an immigrant, besides the fact that he could really use some extra cash."

I just realized how badly Toni was feeling about his lack of proper documentation. He never made a big fuss about it. A few times he had told me about the same dream he kept having, he'd wake up in his house back home and wasn't able to come back here. I should have known better since he said, "Every time I have this dream, I wake up drenched in my own sweat and looking around in horror, trying to figure out where I'm at." But once he'd recognize the furniture, the walls, and his belongings, he'd breathe, relieved that it was just a stupid nightmare.

He and all the immigrants were hoping for the Democrats to win the election. For twenty years, no amnesty on immigration had taken place and there was a big hope something like that would happen. No luck though, because, to everyone's surprise, the Republicans won and they had a totally different approach to the immigration system. No amnesty would take place and different rules and regulations were going into effect soon. Overstaying your visa wasn't considered a felony, or at least not yet, but you could be deported if, for any reason, you landed on their radar. Toni was down for three days when a few friends of Marius's were taken by ICE from their workplace and eventually got deported. I couldn't do anything other than try to make him think positively because things could take a better turn. At this point, nothing could relax him. It turned into anxiety for him and that's why he consulted with a lawyer. She suggested that he get married to an American citizen, if possible; that was the only option for citizenship at this moment. Nothing else would help, unless you were a millionaire investor, another option...

Three months had passed since his family came and we met only once at a hotel nearby. A few times when Eliza and Keli would take their son to the park, we met at his place for an hour or so. I missed him so much and those moments would fly by so fast. I couldn't get enough of him. If I'd met his family, it would be much easier because that way I could spend more time with him and be around more. I was used to having him all to myself anytime I wanted to and this was making me feel sad. I felt like he was changing and being distant. Did they, if not directly, indirectly influence him? He was always tired and sleepy lately. His gaze was distant, lifeless. I wasn't one of those who could hold my thoughts brewing and bothering me for long so I had to ask him why he was acting like that.

"Ema, you deserve someone better, not a guy with a hundred problems on his shoulders."

I tried to make it easy for him by saying, "Let's share the problems together, my love, like we always did. We've been through a lot, this is nothing. We can do it, don't you think?"

"I can't have you meet my family without being divorced," he told me firmly one day. "They will see me as a loser otherwise. Please understand me. I can't believe they are so against it. They haven't said anything openly to me but I feel it. I talked to Keli about you a little, the reason why I picked Chicago, how you helped me, and being special, and one of the most important people I've met in my life. But they don't see it that way unfortunately. In their eyes, I'm so blinded by love and falling into a manipulation of a bored women, and I'm throwing my future away with my own hands."

I was boiling inside but I couldn't be mad or judge them because, after all, I was his choice, not theirs. I wasn't even going to try to influence him in any way but let his free will take its course. If I wasn't "the one" for him, why would I fight? My divorce was about to be final in a few months, tops, but was it even worth it anymore? They didn't like me already, without even seeing or meeting me. No matter what I did and how good I was, to them, in their mind, I was a manipulative, divorced older woman who ruined Toni's life and future. Keli was being diplomatic and implying how naive it was nowadays to pretend that you can love only once in your life.

"How would you know if you don't date a lot of girls, and that's what you do when you're young and single, you explore. That's how you find the one; give those girls a chance, man."

He also told him how truly blinded he must have been not to notice the way the girls at work drooled every time he passed by. There were plenty of young girls, students mostly, working for some extra cash. A few months ago, a new girl started; she was of Arabic descent. She was new to the city and was kind of looking to meet someone. Keli had noticed her interest in Toni. But he was used to that; he knew his charm made him more attractive but he didn't give that any thought or attention. He always thought it wasn't such a good idea to date someone from work and he never did in the past. Every time she needed something or had any questions, Toni responded politely and helped her when he could; kindness was in his nature. It was Keli who was trying to connect them and be the matchmaker. The girl was thirty-three or thirty-four years old, and in her culture, girls have an expiration date; they should have married before hitting their thirties. She left Boston with a one-way ticket, disappointed, heartbroken from her past lovers. When she left her country first to come to America and study, she left in a hurry without much notification, with the help of her mother. If she hadn't left, she would've had to marry her cousin that her father had already picked out for her. But she didn't want him. He called her his on the day he took her virginity by force one day when he found her alone at home. He did that purposely to make sure she belonged to him and him only. It didn't matter to her, she was different from the other Arabic girls; she was full of hopes and dreams in life. She wanted to marry a rich sheik so she could travel the world and maybe live somewhere in the Western world. Don't they all have houses all over the French and Spanish rivieras? If not that, she at least wanted to marry a guy who would somehow fulfill that dream, and none of those cousins of hers, or any boy she knew, could do that.

That's why she went to college, with the hope she would meet a boy up to her standards there, but no sheiks or rich kids were around. Usually their children get educated in the most prestigious schools all over the world. When she got approved to go and study in America after she applied without telling anyone, she felt free already. She so badly wanted to leave that place. Here in America, she was hoping to find the one and, that way, she wouldn't have to hear her mother and aunts reminding her that she was getting old. Twenty-seven and not married; it was making them compare her to other female cousins her age who were about to give birth to child number two by now. Her mother told her once during an argument that she brought nothing but shame to her family for being a single woman that long. People talk, and not necessarily good things. When she arrived in Boston, her most important dream of getting married and starting a family got shattered again.

So far she had a total of six lovers already and, for a Western girl, that is considered an average normal number, but in her culture, she would be labeled a slut. What she realized here was that not all the men you sleep with will give you the ring and want to be together forever. She wasn't madly in love with any of them but she liked them. They treated her well. Then she fell in love with a Moroccan man. It felt like home to be with someone you shared a similar background with—you get each other, you like similar things, you act more like yourself without trying hard to fit in. She focused even more now on the idea of getting married because that biological clock thing started to bother her. And now that she'd passed thirty, it was about time to settle. But she was so unlucky in love. At times she felt like someone must have put a curse on her or something, because that guy who she loved and trusted was the one who broke her heart the most. While being with her, her boyfriend was married to a "good girl" from his country and, now that her papers were ready after a year of waiting, she was coming here. He said they could continue seeing each other because he loved her, she was different, she was fun.

Oh, she left heartbroken for Chicago, thinking that she wasn't good enough to be wife material, but she was fun. What was that supposed to mean? She felt used and low but found her strength, fixed her crown, and decided that in Chicago she would start a new life, totally different from the past, and she was going to be smart dealing with boys now. She had learned a thing or two. First, she invested in her looks. She lightened her hair because, according to the fashion experts, a shade or two lighter warms your physiognomy. She enhanced her eyebrows with microblading, a very modern, costly procedure that gives you the most perfect natural-looking arch. She also did the extended lashes—another lavish procedure but no one would know because, again, they looked so real, like God had blessed you with such features. Botox and little fillers on the lips made her look more youthful and well rested. She loved herself looking like that and it boosted her confidence. What she had learned from living in America and from those boys who played her was that guys were attracted to those independent, outgoing girls, at least in appearance, unlike in her country where no one wants his wife to go to work or do chores driving around all day long. Oh, how good she knew boys now. That's why she went and bought herself a Mercedes—used, of course, with a lot of miles on it, but she wanted it to make a statement. The impression she gave was a beautiful, independent, and successful woman: the whole package. She spent every penny she had saved all these years but for a good cause. The dream of meeting a sheik was long gone, but she could marry a good guy, well-educated with a steady income who could give her the stability she always wanted.

Her coworkers at the pizza place were all Eastern Europeans with degrees in architecture and engineering, but who ended up there for lack of proper documents. They were all on expired visas, basically illegals. She'd heard them joke about how only marriage with an American citizen could save them from being deported if they got caught. She wasn't American yet, but she was in the process of becoming one. When she arrived, she applied for asylum and it was granted immediately, due to the political problems in her country. Every day she was feeding herself more and more with that idea—after all, she was tired of being alone, paying all those bills. Her eyes were on Toni. He seemed like such a nice guy and was easy on the eyes. He was a true gentleman, kind and polite and highly educated in his hometown. She lost her mind over him when Keli told her more things, like that he had his own business—a delivery company that supplied restaurants—owned two trucks, had his own place, and no girlfriend. She didn't know many people here and, heading toward her forties, she wasn't going to let this chance slip from her hands. She was being just flirtatious enough to spark interest and attract guys around her. She wanted to be that new girl at work that everyone admires and wants, but no one was able to get. At lunch breaks, she would sit next to Toni and tactfully ask him questions about his life, and innocently but effectively pay him compliments. She would do this by looking directly into his green eyes, and feel the turbulence it caused. She dressed well and elegantly, wore nice perfume, and was always laughing and smiling, spreading nothing but good, positive energy around Toni.

A few times coworkers joked with them, saying how good they looked together. She would laugh instead of getting mad, thus activating more chemistry. That girl didn't care what people thought or said; her objective was to get close to Toni until they were a couple. She didn't understand half of their conversation because her English wasn't as good as his, but it didn't matter; she'd already caught Toni's attention. He would help her with everything and was being protective. Toni even warned her to be careful and firm with all the Mexicans in the kitchen who'd check her out every time she walked by. She acted all shocked and surprised to find that out when all she'd done was just be friendly and nice to them, but, of course, she'd be more careful in the future. She'd hug him and thank him for all that care and kindness she'd never experienced before and say how touched she was.

There was no denying that Toni was feeling good about it, which is why he mentioned it during a conversation while having a beer with Keli. He knew, of course, and was watching in a way to see how things were progressing, and said "Man, this girl is crazy about you." He was surprised to find that he hadn't asked her out already. The girl, on the other hand, was being very diplomatic since she had decided that Toni was going to be her future husband. She was taking Toni from the inside and began to befriend Eliza. Their apartment was walking distance from the pizza place and Eliza had stopped by a couple of times with her adorable three-year-old son.

The girl told her how much she loved children and couldn't wait to have her own. During those short meetings, Eliza invited the Arabian girl to stop by anytime she wanted to see the little boy. And she did, sometimes showering him with chocolates during these brief visits, sometimes with toys, just enough to leave a good impression. They liked her a lot. Eliza told Toni what a nice and beautiful girl she was.

One day Toni invited me to his apartment. His sister lived in the apartment across the way by now. Luckily, a place became available in that same complex. He seemed nervous and kept looking out of the window at the parking lot. Then, during our conversation, he asked me what I knew about Arabians—their culture, anything. He must have forgotten that, with my intuition, I could figure out that he was up to something without even speaking.

"Besides the fact that their women are very hairy," I said, "I don't know much about them."

He couldn't help laughing at that and got the irony, of course.

"Why did you invite me here, Toni? To break my heart, to make the last comparison? Why? Tell me."

All of a sudden, he said that he had to go somewhere, while looking at his watch and hiding his eyes. Then he mumbled that his sister had invited a couple of friends over and he should be there, they might be here at any moment and...

"And?! Can't you have your girlfriend at your apartment? You don't need permission for that."

"'Girlfriend'? We no longer have that status with each other, Ema: boyfriend/girlfriend."

"Ah, I see. Your status outside these walls is single."

"Truthfully, yes."

Toni smirked cynically. I was boiling inside but I was trying to control my emotions and not pick a fight.

"Are you seeing someone else, Toni? Catching feelings? Please tell me the truth, don't backstab me."

"I wouldn't call it call it anything yet, but I met a girl and it might work. I might start seeing her on a regular basis and get to know her."

"Are you serious? I can't believe this. That hurts. You can be so mean sometimes. Love is the best thing to happen to someone and worth fighting for, and here I am fighting my fight alone, for who? Why are you doing this to me? Didn't I ask you that if you started seeing someone else to please do it when you're completely disconnected from me? When we are totally done and over? You know it would kill me knowing that you are bringing someone new to the apartment I arranged for you—where we first started our love, building our dreams—and worst of all, you living here with someone else. Please don't do this to me. We live so close to each other and it would literally kill me to see you with my replacement, going about your daily routines or driving by, or entering that apartment. Oh, that hurts. There are plenty of apartments, please move to a different one. Please move far away from me, Toni."

"I have nowhere to go, Ema. It wasn't me who wanted things to turn out this way, it was you. Don't you want to see me happy? Look at us. All we do is fight. One day good, the other day fighting. It doesn't work. We can't continue forever like that."

I was numb. I felt lost, like someone had dropped me in the middle of a busy crossroad and I had no idea which direction to go. It was pointless to try to explain things to Toni—that it is cruel to enter someone's life and then leave after you break her into pieces. Did he get it that it was so hard and almost impossible to put those broken pieces back together? People have feelings, people have emotions. I was shattered.

"Ema, you have to understand, you were a special person to me, the most special so far, but things have changed. I have changed."

"When, Toni? When? While I am turning everything upside down to be with you? This isn't right."

I left with my soul crumbling, without thinking at the time that this apartment was once the most loving place to me and would turn into a symbol of my pain...

Chapter 26

That day Ben went to the emergency room with heart attack symptoms. He had chest pain and couldn't breathe. The next day he felt better and more normal, but he had to go through a lot of blood tests and all kinds of other tests to make sure things were okay. I don't know why I called Toni to tell him all this. His response was cold. He said how sorry he felt and begged me to cancel the divorce.

"We are killing him, Ema, don't you see? He never wanted to lose you, otherwise he would have done that long ago."

"How are we killing him? Weren't you the one lecturing me about how wrong it was to live in a loveless marriage? Weren't you the one who told me how wrong it is to live a double life? Do you really think I like adultery and these kinds of adventures? Not at all, in fact. I hate that, that's why I'm fighting to put everything in order and live with dignity. Didn't we both like that, Toni? Tell me please, didn't we?"

"Ah, Ema, enough with the blaming game. You had me, all of me, to yourself. Crazy about you and your disposition. But slowly you killed what we had. And now I'm tired and filled with disappointment. I'm confused. I don't know if I have the strength to fight, and I don't know what I'm fighting for. We loved each other, Ema. We had that kind of love that people rarely have, but

I came to a conclusion that, in life, it's better to be loved than love. It is better to have some peace in your life with someone who loves and cares about you dearly, instead of chaos. It is better to have peace than euphoria that tears your soul in pieces. Years passed by, Ema. My life is passing by. What did I achieve these last few years? What did I do with my life besides bring turmoil into your life and maybe mine as well? Love is overrated. It is not as important as they make it seem. You did the right thing by not coming with me and leaving everything behind. You were smart not to act impulsively."

"Oh, Toni. What are you saying? Our love wasn't worth it? Our feelings weren't worth sacrifices? Are they gone? How can I let go of what I feel for you? That will be like a curse over my head for the rest of my life. Of course I am going to take care of Ben, especially now that he needs me, but is it right for me to continue to live in misery after he gets better? I feel like I owe it to myself to be happy. For years I was hiding the lack of desire to make love to Ben. It was a chore that I was trying to avoid as much as possible and it felt gross doing it. But I was married to him, and that was part of marriage, I guess. I thought that way was easier—he finished faster, and a bunch of questions were avoided. When I avoided it, he would ask if I didn't like him, if I still felt for him, or he'd say 'touch me here' and 'touch me there.' I would close my eyes, not wanting him to read my aversion in them. When he was done, I was released, the torture was over."

"Do you hear yourself, Ema? How long should I wait for you? How long should I suffer? What about my happiness? Why am I always the one to compromise? Maybe we weren't meant to be together. Maybe fate has something different in store for me, and how will I know if I trap myself in that long, endless saga? I want us to be friends only. I don't want this to go on any longer, especially now that he is sick. Take care of him. Bye..."

I couldn't believe how things were spinning out of control in my life, right in front of my eyes. Toni couldn't realize that the reason why he was feeling that way was because we hadn't spent time with each other like we used to. We were used to being with each other for hours and hours. We weren't intimate and this could ruin any relationship, not to mention the pressure from his family against me. But they were doing it in a such a diplomatic way to make Toni believe that he was coming to those conclusions on his own. He was at that age when you start thinking of finding the right person, the one you start a family with and will be happy with for the rest of your life. He was changed for real. When we were on good terms, and we talked about the future, family, and children, he considered finding the right partner the most important thing in life. "Children are a bonus, not an investment," he thought then. Was it maybe because he had started to catch feelings for that girl?

Jealousy was eroding me. I felt pressure in my chest and couldn't breathe. My emotions were now getting all tangled up and taking control. As for my brain, it was totally out of order. I called Toni, and it wasn't me talking but my soul, my heart, my disappointed heart. I was talking, yelling, screaming, not like the other episodes we had in the past, but worse, much worse. I started with:

"Toni, tell me the truth. I want to talk to you. It is necessary that we have a real talk. You're so distant lately and this is hurting me. I miss you so much, don't you understand? Why are you avoiding me?"

He didn't give any explanation because he was afraid of them. Every time we had "the talk," we ended up in each other's arms again. He didn't want that. He wanted to get away from me, to disconnect. But why in that way though? Why like a thief? And what was up with being just friends? Why didn't he need me around?

"No, Toni, no. I want the truth. What we had was nothing?"

"Ema, put it in your mind that what we had was the deepest love I ever felt in my life. But, in life, we find and feel many kinds of loves, and I'm afraid this is not the right one for me. It's destructive."

"Do you love her, Toni?"

"I didn't say I have someone else in my life. I said I met someone with whom it might work. I wouldn't call it love if that makes you feel any better. She just makes me feel good, that's all for now."

"Oh my God, you've been lying to me the whole time. That's why you were avoiding me. You lied, Toni, you betrayed me, you cheater, you. I hate you, oh how much I hate you. How could you do this to me? How long has this been going on?"

"I didn't start anything yet, but we should stop seeing each other for good. I can't deal with your drama any longer."

He blocked me from all social media and I had no way or form of communicating with him. Every day I would wake up with the hope that his heart would mellow out from the absence of me. When you miss someone, you tend to forget their mistakes and all the good memories remain. I was hoping he'd put everything behind him and we would start talking again like two good old friends. When that didn't happen, I was filled with sadness. Sadness turned into anger, and I'd leave him hundreds of voice mails. Those he couldn't block until they were full. He went silent on me. No response, and silence sometimes is the loudest answer you can give someone, but I wasn't in my right mind to understand that. I wanted closure. I wanted to know all the hows and whys.

I asked him to meet me for the last time at a coffee shop so we could talk and shake hands at the end like civilized people do, who once cared for each other. I wanted to hear him tell me face-to-face that he no longer had feelings for me. I wanted him to tell me that he was in love with someone else, if that was the case. I would totally understand him. After all, who understands love better than me? It was going to hurt, I knew that, but the truth hurts only once, a lie hurts every time you remember it. He never responded, just disappeared, like he never existed. And to make things worse, that meant he didn't care. I was destroyed emotionally. I felt like everyone was leaving me—Toni, Ben, myself whom I could no longer recognize. That classy woman with a strong character seemed to be someone who didn't belong to me. That woman who once believed that, if you feel unwanted, leave before you were left, was transformed into someone else who didn't exist anymore. Why couldn't I let him go? Wasn't his silent treatment, his coldness, enough to make me turn around and move on with my life? Was he the only meaningful thing in my life? Why was I sitting with crossed legs in agony, hoping that maybe, just maybe, he'd have a change of heart and come back to me?

Then came the judging, the guilt, the blame. I blamed myself for contributing to our breakup with my lack of communication. I turned our relationship into a constant war and that was unbearable to handle. I didn't leave him any spark to keep the fire of love going. And then there were the circumstances, those freaking circumstances that undermined my happiness. I had everything working against me. But does love really work like that? Don't we want someone to love us unconditionally in life? We want someone to love us even when we are unlovable, or we are hard to love. My mother said that a woman needs a man who loves her more than she loves him. If a man makes your heart race when you see him and you feel euphoric and excited around him, run away; he is not the one. If a man makes you feel calm, warm, and secure in his presence, hold his hand tightly because he is the one for you. She didn't know that the worst battle was the one between what you know is right in your mind and what your heart wants.

Toni started to pick up the phone once in a while. We would talk briefly and from the timber of his voice, I was trying to understand if he was happy or upset. He sounded like the world was coming to an end: down and gloomy. He sounded like he was deeply hurting.

I thought that, if he was in love, he would be hyper, excited, and high on dopamine. People in love are kinder than usual and can't hide their happiness. He was asking me to let him go. He was begging me to help him get out of this misery. He was trying hard to put everything we had behind him. Toni wanted to forget about me, the sooner the better. According to him, I just played with his feelings and, to me, this was just a game. He would call it the biggest disappointment of his life. I wished this was all a bad dream and we would wake up, with him knowing the truth...

Being heartbroken and trying to forget someone puts us in the most vulnerable position where we crave love and attention the most. The Arabian girl was carefully following all the stages Toni was going through. She had attended university in her country; being in America for a few years might have changed her a bit, but her home mentality was very different. Like most of the girls there, she had been programmed since an early age to be obedient to their men and make the best wives someday. They were taught to not raise their voices to them, to present themselves as happy and upbeat, to hide their sadness, and to not lose their class. That's how a girl from a good family would behave. At first sight, she seemed a bit naive, which somehow made her more attractive, but she had learned quickly how to deal with a man, and knew exactly what to do and say to make him go down on his knee and propose quickly. She learned how to let them see what they wanted to see, not who she really was. She was going to marry her prince and make every cousin and every girl in her town jealous. The one she had in mind had no connection with her "filthy" past and now, instead of being the talk of her town for not being married at thirty-four, they would talk about her highly and with envy. She knew that.

Going to work was the best thing for her now. She would make herself ready and spend hours fixing her hair and makeup, changing outfits, yet looking like she was not trying too hard. When she was at work, wearing her smile and having everyone around giving her compliments for her exotic look, she would get close to Toni, and make small talk with him, uninterruptedly looking him in his green eyes. She would touch him innocently while passing each other at work, then apologize politely and act all embarrassed. She would ask Toni about himself, about his childhood stories, find out what kind of music he liked, and act all interested in him only. She would make up beautiful stories about her childhood when he'd ask, and try to explain in her broken English. When he was sitting in the corner looking at his phone, she would send him a song from her country with English subtitles, wanting him to get the message through the lyrics. He had noticed by now that this girl was falling for him and he really liked her as a person, but something kept him from asking her out. He could see her love and desire in her eyes and her gestures.

One day when they were alone, she asked Toni if he had a girlfriend. He looked down instinctively and his cheeks were burning from her piercing eyes staring at him. Toni told her that he had broken up with someone he'd been in a long-term relationship with not long ago. She didn't stop her questions there; she got a bit closer to him and wanted to know why things hadn't worked out between them. He started to tell her things that he hadn't shared with anyone; he told her everything, tearing up at times. Instead of being jealous, she let him talk and let all his hidden pain out, all his lost love and disappointments. She teared up with him at times and told him that this Ema was a lucky woman to be loved like that by a guy like him.

"I thought those things only happened in books and movies and I didn't know that men like you existed. I would give anything to experience and have a love like that in my life."

Toni was touched by her words. He felt appreciated, worthy, and when he walked her out to her car, they hugged and they kissed, on the lips. He was so vulnerable and hurt from what was going on in his life that, to his surprise, this felt good. He had no idea that she was playing her role of making him fall for her. At that age, she was not complete as a woman, without a husband, without children. That was the only thing that mattered in life: having a family, having children. Those were your treasures. It didn't matter much who the husband was at this point. It was good enough to be a good person, a hard worker, and wanting a family. It didn't have to be crazy love. His love would be enough regardless. Her mom and her aunts told her that love gets deeper after you have children together. First you marry that nice guy and then you work on your marriage and make yourself attractive to him. You work on your bed, on your look, and bring the families—his and yours—closer. Friendship between them is one of the best ways to bond.

In a few words, it was like a system that worked. So first you attract the man, make him fall for you and believe that there is no other girl like you. Never sleep with him before marriage, which is going to make him want you more and burn with desire. Give him the impression that he is your world and you belong only to him in life and can't wait to have his children. After this, the next step is the families mingling together at family events, activities, and becoming this big harmonious group. Show respect for your man, his people, and things will get better and better, just like her mom and aunts did.

He kissed her on her lips. The system was working. The next day she looked distracted and not as enthusiastic as usual. Toni noticed that and asked her when she was close by if everything was okay. The girl burst into tears and apologized in a soft voice for what had happened last night. That was something that she asked him to forget about and would never happen again. It was very immature on her part. She asked him if he could please not judge her character by it. It was simply a moment of weakness. It was the first time she had allowed a boy to kiss her without being in a relationship. Toni felt her warmth in those tears and heartfelt words, but he knew she didn't mean it. He knew she was a good and appropriate girl brought up in a strict environment with rules to follow. Because she told him never again didn't mean that she wanted him to stop. Instead of apologizing back to her, he came up with exactly what she wanted.

"I don't know what will happen in the future, and I can't promise you anything yet, but would you let me take you out to dinner sometime? Would you?"

She tried to play hard to get at first by saying, "I don't know if I should or not..."

Toni, trying to help her with her answer and, making things easier with humor, assured her that, up to this point, he hadn't eaten another human. She laughed and kissed him on his cheek, and that was a yes. After that, she was busy working, waiting tables and making Toni miss her...

Toni didn't pick up the phone and didn't answer me anymore. I left him voice messages until it was full. He didn't care about my desperation to talk to him or meet him somewhere for closure.

Did I mean nothing to him? Where had all the promises gone? How can you tell someone one day "you are the most important person in my life and no one can come between us" and the next day forget she exists?

One day my phone rang. My heart was beating so fast once I recognized his number, I thought it would jump out of my chest. At the moment, I thought he couldn't resist me any longer and things would go back to the way they were again. I was all nice and warm to him, and he, on the other hand, was distant and cold.

"I got fired," he said. "Someone called the manager, some lawyer's wife who found out that not only don't I have the proper documentation to work there, but that I don't even have a valid driver's license. She called to ask how a company like that could hire illegals who have driver's licenses given to them just to go from point A to point B, not work as a delivery driver. She threatened that she would call the authorities, ICE specifically, if this problem isn't fixed immediately, for public safety."

"Oh, Toni," I said, without knowing how important this particular pizza place was to him. "Don't you worry, darling, there are plenty of pizza places who would hire you on the spot. I thought something terrible happened, this is nothing to worry about. It's not like you lost a job at NASA," I said sarcastically, trying to make him smile if not laugh. "It's not the end of the world. It's just not a good era for immigrants these days and this is happening all across the country."

"NOOOO!" he yelled. "I did not want to lose this job. I was able to pay all my rent with those three days working there."

"I know, love, but sometimes things like this happen. There's nothing you can do but look for another one."

"Please don't call me 'love' again. Did you do this? You're the only one who knows so many details about me."

"Toni, are you out of your mind?" I said without hiding my anger and shock that he could even think that. "Why would I do this to you? I want to see you happy, not stressed out. I can't believe you'd think that. It's low. Why are you so attached to that place who kicked you out in the first place? As I said, there are hundreds more around. They all pay the same."

"Why? Do you want to know why I feel like that? Because I was humiliated in front of my friends, coworkers, and my brother-in-law when my manager called me into his office. Then I had to tell everyone that I was fired because of improper paperwork. It is true that I didn't lose a NASA job, and it's just a fucking pizza place, but wasn't I good enough to work even there? I don't know why I think that you have something to do with it. Maybe you were fueled by jealousy and wanted me fired from there."

I wanted to hang up on him so badly and let him choke on his words, because I didn't need to listen to his brutal accusations, but I had waited so long for this phone call. He continued to talk, taking out all his anger with a calm tone, where you can feel in the words how deeply hurt he was.

"My brother-in-law was right when he said 'you are destroying your life going after someone who is already married and belongs to someone else. You could have found someone who you could get your papers and start a family with instead. Why? There are plenty of fish in the sea.' Tell me, Ema, did you call my work?"

"Toni, I refuse to answer that. I can't believe you have the audacity to ask. I'm not your enemy and to do something like that is vengeful. What is happening with you, my love?

What is happening with you, my love? I know I'm not an angel and never pretended to be one. But I thought you knew me better."

"Ah, you. You destroyed me, ruined me as a man. You kept me around like a dog tied up. You didn't care when I'd toss and turn in my bed at night trying to fight the thought that you were sleeping next to someone else. Why did I fall for that? How did I agree to such a thing and allow myself to be played for a fool? But I know why I put up with everything. I did it because I loved you so much. I loved you like no one else in my life. I search for you in every woman I meet and I don't really want to find you again, I just want to feel how I felt for you. I have told you often that I would never be able to love again the way I loved you, but I won't let you win. I have promised myself that I will love again. I will love who I want to love. I will choose carefully. I will love someone who deserves me and is dedicated. Someone who wants to have only me in her life. I will love someone who will take me as I am, without money or status, to love me when I am nobody."

"That was me, Toni. I loved you for who you are. I still do." And tears were rolling down my cheeks. I tasted the salt in them when they entered my mouth as I spoke.

"Oh, please. Don't you dare continue expressing emotions like that. You had me, all to yourself, but you lost me, Ema. You lost me once and for all. Now let me live my life in peace. Please do not contact me anymore. Pretend I don't exist, and I will do the same. You don't exist." Click. He hung up.

My knees got weak. I was crawling over on my stomach because it was hurting everywhere. I knew why I was feeling like that—all the symptoms and the causes because I was a psychologist—but I couldn't avoid those feelings...

I followed my daily routine, wearing the mask of a woman who had everything going well in her life. I involved myself in many activities to keep my mind busy. My face had gotten noticeably thinner, and I might have lost some weight because my clothes were flowing freely on my body. I started going out with my friends, simple things like having a coffee or grabbing a sandwich somewhere. I started going to painting classes more often and pouring my heart into the canvas. Then I would rigorously attend Zumba classes. As busy as my schedule was, when I was left alone with myself, I had to deal with my pain. Heartbreak is not something as pretty or poetic as they make it seem in songs. It's listening to heartbreaking songs until three in the morning. It's feeling like you're going to die in the middle of the street filled with people.

You feel like you see the face of the person who left you in every car that passes by. You might start feeling better for a few days in a row until one day you feel his ghost lips kissing your spine and giving you chills. Then you start choking on the memories that bring back his ghostly presence. It's waking up in the middle of the night screaming his name while you were dreaming that he came back to you, then feeling a pain like a tank hit you. So many song lyrics have romanticized heartbreak. But it is not true. It is a lie. Heartbreak is not something almost beautiful like in the songs; instead it's the worst feeling someone can experience and you don't wish it on your worst enemy.

One day we were in our cars at the stop light waiting for the light to change. Toni was with his brother in law Keli and when our eyes met, he turned his head to the other side like he didn't know me. This was the saddest thing. Two people who know each other in every detail: know each other's secrets, their fears, things they love or hate, what their favorite thing is and what isn't, but are now complete strangers. They pass by each other and pretend they've never met, when, in fact, they know every part of their body, every hidden little scar. I never knew how deeply I was in love until I felt like I was drowning and needed to look for the shores. While he blocked me from everything, the old-fashioned way of mailing letters still existed. I wrote him short apologies, which I regretted later. I didn't get any answer from him, just silence. Two months had passed and I couldn't take it anymore. I decided to go and pay him a visit at his apartment. I was hoping that maybe when he saw me at the door, my presence would make him realize how much he missed me and my humbleness would touch his heart. Time apart does wonders sometimes and maybe he'd invite me inside like he used to not long ago, though it felt like ages. My heart wasn't ready to forget him; it was impossible for me to give up. I parked my car and, for a moment, I let the fresh air from the open window hit my face. I was all nostalgic for the days when I used to go there any time that I wanted to. I looked around and recognized some neighbors' cars. They were the same people I would wave to here and there whenever we crossed paths.

Toni lived on the second floor and the blinds were wide open so you could see clearly when he walked. I got all teared up when I saw his silhouette moving, and "Oh, Toni, I love you" slipped from my lips. I couldn't wait to see his reaction through the window when I called him on his phone by pressing *67 first since he had blocked me. I googled how to call someone who has blocked me. It would show private, of course, but he probably knew it was me calling. He didn't pick up even though I was able to hear it ringing through the open window. I called again. This time a girl who wasn't too tall with light brown hair picked it up and gave it to him. He made a gesture to forget it and leave it alone. I thought my blood was moving too fast through my arteries and was going all the way down to my feet. I was shocked. Then I called that phone nonstop until he figured that I must be outside and watching, so, instinctively, he came to the window. He saw me and tried to close the blinds. The brown-haired girl opened them and she was already pissed off and asked him, "Why is she here? Didn't you tell her to leave us alone? Call the police. Why are you protecting her? Call them. She is stalking you, don't you understand? I want her arrested!" she yelled.

Then half her body was outside of the window and she started yelling at me.

"Hey, leave. Leave us alone, don't you understand you're this psycho ex and he doesn't want you? Maniac woman. Tell her, Toni. Did you tell her? Call the police!" she screamed.

Apparently every time that I had called him from my blocked number and he didn't answer, she must have been present. In her eyes, I was this crazy ex that they couldn't get rid of. I felt like my organs were leaving my body and falling out one by one in this big, well-lit parking lot. I had never experienced that kind of pain in my life. It wasn't only emotional; it was physical too.

I don't know how I left the car and I found myself on the stairway that takes you to his door. Toni was coming down the stairs toward me. He told me to stay and wait for him. The girl, his girl, was screaming from the window to get everything recorded and on tape as proof for the police. I was confused. What did the police have to do with me? What kind of danger would I put them in that they were afraid of me? I thought I was the one who needed help to make it out alive and get the hell out of this parking lot, because I was too weak to walk.

I turned around, hyperventilating and sobbing my way to the car. I couldn't leave there fast enough. I finally reached my car and peeled out with my tires screeching. Toni was standing there quietly recording me leaving with his phone. Me, the criminal psycho woman. I pitied him. Once I was on the open road, I started screaming like crazy. I cursed my fate, I cursed myself for being such immature. I cursed Toni with all my heart for all the pain he had caused me, for his betrayal and his backstabbing. It had hurt me because he was the person I loved the most in life. The person I trusted the most was the one who had lied and disappointed me. He left me alone when I needed him the most.

Toni called me, probably because she pushed him to do it to make her feel better. She hadn't stopped yelling and took his phone and told me to leave them alone for good, for their happiness. She didn't bother to question why this normal-looking woman, at least in appearance, had gone there. Was there any unfinished business between me and him she didn't know about? How come Toni hadn't told me about her? It didn't bother her that Toni, without being healed from a breakup, had jumped quickly into a new serious relationship. But that didn't seem to matter to her; or worse, that was a perfect opportunity for her to take advantage of his vulnerability. He was hurt and only by showering him with love and making him believe he had found the right girl for life would he forget the past. All she cared and wanted was to not have his ex around, period. Everything else would work smoothly as she had planned.

She must not have known that when someone enters into a new relationship too quickly after a breakup it is just a coping mechanism to forget. What you feel and experience is the imitation of lost love. But most likely it is not true love, and has nothing to do with it. Ninety-nine percent of these relationships end up in breakups shortly after they start. Men are as brittle as women, only they cope differently with pain. It's very common that, before they even break up with someone they loved but it's no longer working, they jump into the arms of the first woman who gives them attention. This is because they feel powerless to deal with separation. They want support.

I had no energy to fight her. I let her air out her anger, and I couldn't make the connection between her and Toni. How had a guy like him gone for a girl like her? Then he took the phone from her. His voice penetrated my soul. All I could say through my tears was:

"Why, Toni? Why did you do this to me? What did I do to you to deserve this? Why didn't you tell me the truth? Didn't I deserve some honesty and sincerity? What happened to the promise that no other woman could ever separate us? That 'if I don't end up with you, I will never marry again. If I give a ring to someone, that will be only you.' Did you forget those? Do you love her, Toni?"

He didn't talk, and I felt like he was hurting too. I felt his war with himself and that he was trying to hold in his emotions, which were gathered up and could explode at any moment. Not anger, or hate, but feelings that he was trying to push down inside and kill them there.

"It's too late for everything, Ema. Take care of yourself and please forget about me."

"Why haven't you called the police all this time if I have been bothering you?"

"You know very well how I have protected your privacy and identity. She knows everything about you and why I came to Chicago, but not who you are, not your name. I have done this for the sake of what we had, even though we have talked about you, or us, for hours sometimes."

The girl asked him to speak in English with me. She yelled again hysterically, asking why he was being so nice to me. I'm pretty sure Toni took that as a sign of love.

"Did you already forget what she has done to you?"

"Ema, I have to end our conversation. She has no part in it, and I have no reason to hurt her feelings."

"Are you happy, Toni?"

"No."

He disappeared with a click. Nothing could calm my hurting soul. I was confused. Why was he with her if he wasn't happy? Now I had no choice but to give up. He had replaced me with someone new. He has her anytime he wants to, where he wants to. Even if he ever thought about or missed me, he was going to hug and kiss her to remind himself that I am just someone from the past. Even if sometimes I entered his dreams and ruined his sleep, he would turn around and spoon hug her for the same reasons. No one knows how painful it is to lose someone special in life until the moment you fall on your knees and beg God to heal and mend your broken heart. You beg God to heal your mind for a new beginning, a new start. It is that kind of pain when you feel like you have nothing left to lose...

Another month went by. I had no idea what was going on with Toni and his life. I never passed by his street. I was broken, shattered, slow, and I felt like I was a hundred years old. I don't remember much about what I did on those days. It was a mixture of sleepless nights, no appetite, and the movements of a zombie. I was on the edge constantly. Someone did something wrong to me everywhere I went, or that was my impression at least. Not to mention those idiots who'd cut me off in traffic and I'd curse them. Ben was getting on my nerves more than ever, but why he was putting up with me, I don't know. Toni was impossible to get out of my mind. Every day I would mentally picture his funeral, but he had some superpowers and would come out alive again.

Sometimes I'd burst out crying for no reason. Sometimes I'd be good for a few days, thinking that I was going to get through this, but then I'd hear a song on the radio that would put me in such a sad mood. Sometimes I would get a burst of happiness out of nowhere and think that this would be the day Toni would call to tell me that he was no longer with the Arabian girl and it was a total mistake. I was waiting for the phone to ring and could picture him saying how much he missed me. I pictured him apologizing and me forgiving him. The image of all this was so real that I thought it had already happened; none of this happened. It was just a cruel mirage of my imagination. Toni had disappeared from the horizon...

My job become my escape from reality. All my focus was there. One day I had a meeting that was so productive and I felt satisfied after all the hard work I had put into it. I was able to sign a two-year contract that was very beneficial to the company I worked for. Rumors were that I was about to be promoted to director. When I walked out of the glass doors of the building and heard the echo of my heels, I remembered that I hadn't eaten anything. Lately my appetite was gone and feeling hungry was a good sign that I was getting better. I Google searched the nearest restaurant where I could grab a bite. Wherever you go, there is never a shortage of restaurants. This town was about an hour away from my home and it was almost like a getaway for me. I'd never been there before, and it gave me this strange good feeling. Maybe because I was always trying to run away from my feelings and emotions, I felt connected to unfamiliar places. I was trying to escape from the everyday routine and who knew that just driving to the next town could do it. I decided to enjoy my warm and toasted sandwich with a hot, strong coffee to open my eyes and get some energy. Toni popped up in my mind. I couldn't make him go away. If we were on good terms, or friendly at least, he would have been the first one I would've called to share my project and the contract. It was something similar to what I was doing when I met Toni. This time it had to do with funds given to offer psychological services to abused and traumatized women and children refugees. This was another part of why I missed Toni terribly. I missed our conversations, our debates—some argumentative ones, some challenging, but they were meaningful. It used to be so pleasant to talk with him for hours and hours. I didn't lose only the love of my life, but my best friend too. If only I could go back and erase what had happened, if only I had one more chance, I would do anything to never lose Toni again.

I was drowning my thoughts while scrolling through Facebook pictures and quietly sipping my coffee. Toni's sister's profile showed up as one of the suggested ones. I clicked it; I don't know why. I almost fell off my chair when I checked the pictures she was tagged in. Those pictures killed me. I noticed the Arabian girl in those albums. How could this be real? Then I clicked on the pictures of that girl. She was in a white dress and had white flowers in her hands. Toni was standing next to her with a big smile on his face. Those pictures ended any bit of hope that he and I would get back together. In one of the pictures were two hands—hers with a not- too-big diamond ring holding Toni's hand, which also had a ring. One picture was probably taken at city hall where they were looking at each other while the judge was marrying them. Another picture was a celebration taken at a restaurant. She and Toni were holding wineglasses and looking toward the person who was taking the pictures.

The girl looked really happy. She had done it. Her formula had worked and faster than she had expected. It was magical. In a few months—maybe two or three—she had made him go down on one knee and propose. Her Facebook page was private, except for those albums. It was like she left them public on purpose. Maybe for me to see, or someone from her past. Could be for her friends and cousins who she doesn't talk to anymore and she wanted them to see how lucky she was. It didn't matter who she had left them open for; I wished I'd never seen them.

Oh God, he had gotten married so quickly. But why? What was all the rush? Was she pregnant? Was he afraid of being deported? I got up and was walking as fast as I could to my car. I lay down on the car seat with my arms around my stomach, trying to ease the pain. For the first time, I wanted to hate him so much. I wanted to forget him, to turn him into dust, and get him out of my mind. How much time would I need to forget him? The least he could have done was not bring her to our apartment. Not make love to her in the bed we bought together. Did she know that bed had gotten wet so many times from our passionate lovemaking? I had left a part of me there. Did she feel that energy? I was going crazy...

"Love is short, forgetting is so long."
Pablo Neruda

Life goes on, no matter what. I would've done anything possible to get out of that stage I was in. I was not in a good state emotionally, psychologically, and physically. I should have started to take care of myself and my family. No one knew what I was going through. No one knew the demons I was fighting off. I was in a war zone and would start my day fighting them. They wouldn't stop and I would fall asleep fighting. I also woke up in the middle of the night from fighting them in my dreams. This was a process and I couldn't avoid going through it. I often wondered if I was ever going to be normal again and get myself out of this hell. I would read, to the point of being obsessed, articles about breakups and healing afterwards, or how to survive them. There were things that I already knew but it felt like I was discovering them for the first time. Maybe it was too late for me to get healed or maybe I was too deep in my misery and nothing seemed to help. For hours I would read articles and stories, which seemed to ease my pain, even if it lasted only a few hours. I found one so relatable it was like I wrote it myself:

"She loved you, but you broke her heart. Instead of loving her and creating something beautiful for both of you, you did the opposite. This hurts, and do you know why? Because she did nothing to deserve the pain you caused her? Unfortunately, she didn't dodge the bullet that went straight to her heart, not a millimeter higher or lower. Her heart exploded in a million little pieces. I don't even know where to start with the list of what you have caused her. Sometimes I ask myself if you feed on the misery that you cause others? Do you feel better about yourself when you break a woman down to the lowest level she has ever been? You didn't care how she felt in the moment you turned your back on her. You never cared to see that your behavior might have a destructive effect on her, and all she wanted was to be with you and love you endlessly. Nothing is worse than falling for the wrong guy. It can ruin you psychologically to be betrayed by the person who supposedly loved you the most. We change after a breakup and sometimes become unrecognizable. When our heart gets broken like that, a transformation happens within us because the lessons learned from it change us to the core. You turned her into a woman who can't trust anyone because she trusted you, but look how that ended up. If she was a little bit smarter, if she hadn't gone that deep with you, and if she didn't believe that you were a good one, her heart wouldn't have been broken like that. She trusts no one anymore. She now keeps one foot in and one outside the door just in case. Since you left her, she protected her heart. She built those tall, thick walls around it that no one could climb. It will take a long time for her to invite someone inside, if she even decides to again. By now she knows that the only person she can trust is herself. She trusted you but you pulled the chair out from under her when she was about to sit so you let her fall down. It was you who made her not trust anyone. The worst part is that she experienced all this while giving you everything. It didn't mean anything to you and so she learned that the only person

THE SINS OF MRS. EMA

she can count on is herself. She gave up on love. True love was the most important thing in her life. In fact it was the only thing worth living for. But she changed her mind and she doesn't want that anymore. She learned that love hurts, thanks to you. You showed her the dark side of it and that's how she'll see it from now on. She said goodbye to love and doesn't want to love or be loved. This chapter in her life is closed and, most likely, permanently. Anyway, she also learned how to laugh when she wanted to scream instead. She put on a smile while everything was crumbling inside her. She wasn't very good at it at first, but life has a funny way of teaching us things we never thought we could learn. She learned how to bottle up her feelings. No one knew how she felt. When she feels like she wants to scream and let the pain all out, she smiles, because she is terrified that if she lets herself go down that road, she won't be able to pick up the pieces of her breaking. She doesn't tell anyone how she feels. She doesn't ask for help and when she is asked, she says 'I'm fine.' No other explanations, only that short sentence with the hated big lie. But that sentence has a million tears inside, a million broken pieces of her, a million emotions. She could be everything at that moment but fine wasn't one of them. It was the most untruthful thing she had ever said. She was once the most fun woman to be around. She was happy and believed in the goodness in people. She believed that love could save the world. You told her the opposite. Her love must not have been big enough to save a person as bad as you. You transformed her into a different creature. She is just a corpse that breathes, eats, walks, talks but is without a soul. She is cold and can't feel love. She doesn't have those warm emotions that humans usually have; even her blood runs ice cold through her veins. Her smiles and her happiness are gone. She lost them all with you. You sucked her into your darkness and then you left her there. You left her without any ray of light coming through her soul..."

Chapter 27

When I went to see my dentist for a routine cleaning, he asked me if everything was okay. Kris had been our family dentist for quite a while. He was Albanian and came to America when he was a young kid. Not only was he fluent in Albanian but he was very much involved with the events of our community in Chicago. That's where we met him, at one of those fundraising events. He had the height of a basketball player, was enthusiastic, and had a very cheerful nature. The first impression you get from him is that he has never had to worry about a thing in his life. He had a full head of thick, black, unruly curls that moved like waves every time he talked with his hands.

Kris tried to change my noticeably sour mood by paying me a compliment. He told me that I had lost some weight and I looked even prettier like that. I couldn't even fake a smile but he didn't take offense. He knew that we were going through a long and complicated divorce, but since he was the dentist of everyone in our family, he stayed neutral. Only once he joked about it and mentioned that our divorce was becoming like the one in the movie *War of the Roses*, which is, in fact, based on a true story. I smiled when I found out that this was the longest divorce process in history and took twenty-one years. It took all those years because they couldn't agree how to share their assets. More money, more problems, and a longer, agonizing process. That's what I tried to explain to Toni in the past but he didn't get it. Kris and Ina got along well. He had seen her since she was a little girl and, not only that, but Ina totally believed that her beautiful teeth were healthy thanks to him. He was indeed an excellent dentist and very humble at the same time. When people would praise him in his presence, he would joke around, since he was so tall, and say:

"If it was up to me, I would have been a Chicago Bulls player, but my family is all a bunch of dentists. They don't know how to do anything else and they made me go to dental school. It's almost like a family tradition now." Kris was like a good giant, like a trustworthy teddy bear, and that day he gave me the ability to express myself to him like an old friend. At first, he recommended I see a friend of his, a very good psychologist, if I needed to talk to someone.

"Even psychologists can use a psychologist sometimes," he said.

But who could listen to me better than him and give me a shoulder to cry on?

Another month passed by and Ben's health was deteriorating. Most of his recent blood tests were uncovering many underlying health issues he had.

Kris suggested that I go easy on him and give him attention and care with kindness because he was in a critical point at this moment in his life. He even mentioned that delaying the divorce for a while might be a good idea and I agreed with him on that. I was already feeling so bad for him and felt guilty. I felt like the stress I caused him lately could have been the reason he got sick. Maybe he wasn't as strong as I thought and couldn't handle this change in his life. You can love someone without being in love with them. That was my case. I didn't care to continue with the divorce any longer. From the moment I broke up with Toni, it didn't matter to me. I didn't care which house I'd live in, or which house Ben would take—nothing mattered anymore.

Toni was right when he asked me to leave everything behind and go to him, because no material things and money in the world could measure up to love or replace it. I must have feared love and thought it was romanticized. That's why I wanted proof and more proof to make sure it was the right thing to do, but nothing ever seemed enough. Some people smoke and die from it, some drink and die from it, maybe some die from a breakup. Can you really die from a broken heart? What are the statistics? I've heard you can, and I hoped it wasn't true...

Ben's behavior had changed lately, for the better. He was much nicer, kinder, and without even a trace of his natural arrogance left. To my surprise, he was calm and appreciative. In more than one case he told me how lucky he was to have me to himself all his life and he wished he'd realized this earlier. I thought that was one of his manipulative tactics, like the Trojan horse kind, and didn't pay much attention to it. I would give him that cold, it's-too-late kind of look. But despite how I felt, I continued to take care of him, prepare his healthy meals, remind him to take his medications on time, and stuff like that. His doctor gave him the ultimatum to change his diet and eating habits immediately because his arteries weren't looking good. They were all clogged up and would most likely need stents very soon.

Ina was living her perfectly happy life in college and having a good, successful year. I had reached that phase in life when you have a sense of gratefulness for what you've achieved, for the way your child has turned out, and, in a way, we all seemed content and balanced at the moment. But in the meantime, there was no way I could forget Toni. I gave up trying to kick him out of my mind and heart. I left him there and learned how to live with my constant pain. I'd be good for a moment, a few hours, or maybe even a day, but then the lyrics of some song playing on the radio would be enough to trigger an outburst. Lately I'd noticed that most of the songs were heartbreaking ones and seemed to be written specifically for me.

I tried to stop myself from loving Toni because trying to hate him was impossible. Unfortunately, love has nothing to do with logic. Love was like a massive, moving substance that ran through my veins just like the blood that flows. He was a part of me and no matter what he put me through, I couldn't separate him from myself. At times I was mad at myself that I couldn't hate him, which would have made my life easier. And to make things worse, I wasn't mad at him. He wasn't mine and I wasn't his, that's all. I had no more hopes that maybe, just maybe, he would come back to me. All I had with were the memories, and only the good ones, which made my soul soft, brittle, and about to break at any moment. The good memories were so vivid and didn't seem they were going to fade away. Time had no impact on them whatsoever. Sometimes I would get this nostalgia and I would die to see a memento of him somewhere. It was very painful to miss someone you can't have. But, on the other hand, it's lucky to miss someone so much because it meant that you had someone special worth missing in your life.

Many torturing thoughts would cross my mind often. Did he ever think of me, or was I just someone from the past now? All that anger had left me once I found out the truth. I wasn't mad at him anymore. Most of the time I was even able to justify his behavior. The girl he was with was the one I never thought of. She left me with a bitter taste. If she had acted differently maybe I wouldn't feel this way. But no, she didn't care that I had unfinished business with Toni. All she wanted was me gone from his life. Typical behavior of a girl who knows she can have a man, a husband, for a long time or forever because of certain circumstances, but deep down she knows another woman has his heart. I wanted the best for Toni either way and I would never, ever interfere with their life. I came to the conclusion that this was my fate and that's how it was meant to be. I also opened my heart with my hands toward the universe to allow myself to love again, to love more. Love is kind, love is life...

Coincidentally, I saw Toni a couple of times around the neighborhood. One of those times was in heavy traffic and I was behind his car. I had no idea it was him until I recognized his license plate and my heart started to beat fast and my hands started shaking. He wasn't alone, but I only saw him. The irony of fate—to go from two people once crazy in love to two strangers in traffic. I couldn't figure out what had made Toni marry her. He was as deep as an ocean and likes to find depth in others. That girl not only didn't seem his type, but her English was limited to communicate at that level. We knew everything about each other, all shades of our souls. We knew each other's tastes and all our likes or dislikes. Did she know that he poured olive oil on anything he ate and a lot of it? Or that he preferred pasta over rice? He wasn't crazy about sweets but liked chocolates and liked wine better than beer. He loved bread. He used only white bedsheets, just like me. We both liked the ocean but he hated the heat. But now that didn't really matter. It was over, a closed chapter.

Another time we coincided on the stoplight waiting for the light to turn green. It looked like he was looking somewhere far away and was kind of lost in his thoughts. I am not sure if he saw me, but he didn't seem happy and didn't have his usual Bluetooth in his ear. When we were together, he never took it off because we would talk nonstop all day, even when we'd meet every day. Maybe he didn't need to talk to her constantly since he had her at home day and night. I don't know why I would tire myself out with all these senseless thoughts.

One day I saw him on my street, right where I make a right turn to go home. I had no other way around but he did. He didn't have to cross that road, especially with her in the car, knowing I pass by there a few times a day at least. I thought he did that purposely. I couldn't stop myself from leaving him a message with a quiet tone in which I said, "If someone tries to make his ex jealous, it means that he is not over her. Don't you think you hurt me enough, Toni? Do you really have to parade on my street when you have ten other alternative roads? I hope you're happy."

He didn't answer, but I also didn't see him there anymore. We crossed paths again on a different road, looking just like two strangers in traffic, no doubt.

Chapter 28

One morning I was surprised to see Ben's car still in the driveway. I thought maybe he'd taken a different one to work, but no, all of his cars were there. He usually left for work early in the morning way before I woke up. I thought he must have taken a day off and that would be record-breaking because he never took a day off. Even when he got sick, he couldn't wait to go to his office. Work was life for him, the most meaningful thing. I went looking for him downstairs on the first floor, but he wasn't there. Also I didn't smell the aroma of coffee he usually makes every morning. It was an eerie kind of quiet. The TV wasn't on either, another part of his morning routine.

"Ben!" I called but got no response.

I opened his office door and didn't see him. I entered inside and there he was, lying down on the couch.

"Ben, are you okay?" He wasn't responding. I shook him and yelled out loud, "Ben, wake up!" He felt cold.

"Oh my God, Ben!" I screamed, panicked by now. "Talk to me, please!"

I picked up the phone and dialed 911 with my shaky hands. I had shivers going through my body and I was in disbelief that something was wrong with him. I told them how I found my husband and to hurry up because he was not opening his eyes. I tried to warm him up by hugging him and kissing him through my tears, but nothing changed. In a few minutes, which seemed like hours to me, the paramedics came and, after they did their examination, said that he had passed away, possibly from a heart attack.

"Oh no, Ben. Why did you leave us so soon? You had many more years left for you to be here. You can't leave like that. What did you see in this life besides working hard? Only work and the problems I have caused you." I felt so guilty, like I had committed a murder.

"Oh, could you have lived longer if I loved you more? Or maybe it would have been better if you had another woman by your side, someone who deserved and loved you enough. Oh God, I made you suffer, I destroyed you. Why in the world did you stick with me when you could have been more selfish and found your own happiness. Maybe you would still be alive today."

I was crying with pain and tears from a guilty conscience. While crying out loud in Albanian, the paramedic had to tap me on my shoulder so they could take him with them. That was a terrifying moment, knowing that this was going to be his last time leaving this house and never coming back again. He was gone, forever...

Losing Ben was like the last kick to knock me downhill. I took care of the preparations for the funeral services and wanted to give him the best funeral ever, if that makes any sense at all. The man I once tried so hard to run away from, and as far and as fast as I could, was the one I was missing deeply. How could this even be possible? He was the person who I couldn't stand being together with for more than five minutes, but somehow he never turned his back on me, even when that was what I wanted. He was the backbone of my life but I couldn't realize that earlier.

Ina was devastated by the loss of her father. He wasn't like those typical fathers to take her to Spanish or piano lessons, but he had provided for her to have everything she ever wanted or needed in life. She was his princess. He made her feel secure and protected and she knew that she was the apple of her father's eye. A few cousins of Ben came to give their last goodbyes and were giving her all their support and warmth to ease her pain. Everyone was saying nothing but good things about him, even his "enemies" who couldn't stand Ben when he was alive. But that's normal and usual. Once someone dies, all their bad qualities aren't mentioned anymore. Ben left behind a world that he would call dirty and dark. He left behind everything he cared for—his family, his wealth—and took with him only a chic suit and shovels of dirt. He took with him the blessing of the priest and prayers of everyone for him to rest in peace. He took with him the tears and pain of his daughter who loved him dearly, and mine...

Through this whole process, Kris showed me what a true friend he really was. He never left our side during those difficult moments and was a great help in many ways. Thanks to his natural good sense of humor, he was the right person to have around to keep up our positive vibes.

"It is a light at the end of the tunnel, Ema, and if not, you can set the tunnel on fire to light it up."

I didn't call Toni to let him know that Ben had passed way. It was pointless. I didn't think he'd care. We were two complete strangers now. I almost died and came back to life but he didn't care. He never asked, or apologized for what he'd caused me, and I thought he should have. He was the reason I went through hell and back. It takes two to tango. I had seen many breakups, but they would still be there and check up on each other, as an act of kindness. Nothing romantic, not as an attempt to get back together either, because there was a reason it didn't work out. But just to not be cold and act like a coward toward someone they once loved. They would end up staying friends, and I wasn't as lucky in that sense.

A few days after the ceremonies and all the guests had left, I had to deal with Ben's attorney and life insurance agency. Ben left me in such great financial shape that I didn't have to worry at all or change my lifestyle. I was, by all means, a very rich woman. I should have found some comfort in that but instead it made the hole in my soul deeper. We couldn't find the common language and communication with each other when he was alive, but somehow he was the person who took care of my well-being until the day he died, and even after his death. A few days before he was gone forever, he had mentioned to me in a soft and warm voice the real reason why he was dragging out the divorce. He was so sure that, one day, I was going to realize that the deteriorated road I was taking had terrible consequences. He wanted to be there for me to pull me up and hold me when I was about to fall. He said that it almost killed him knowing that I was never in love with him. As for the assets that he was supposedly fighting over, they had no real value to him.

"What good will money do me if I lose you, if I don't find you at home making that delicious food and laughing with that best kind of laughter with our daughter? Ema, I gave you a house but you gave me a home. Regardless how everything turned out, you are the most beautiful woman to me, my best friend, and you know I don't have many. I still think you're a good wife and a wonderful mother. Unfortunately, any man can see and value those qualities in you. I realize that we can't make someone love us no matter what we do and no matter how much we love them. That's why I want you to be happy and do what's best for you, my sinful Ema. Maybe it wasn't your fault I might have been a difficult person to love."

I suspiciously thought he must have had a few drinks and this was the alcohol talking, but then he continued...

"The kind of love your soul craves and you are looking for, it's an illusion. It does not exist. True love is a commitment; it's forgiveness, it's caring because it can't be any other way. If you want to see who loved you more in life, take a look at who forgave you the most."

"Why did you cheat on me, Ben? Why didn't you make me love you?" I replied, all aggravated because his words made me feel really bad.

"Ah, the man's betrayal is so different from the woman's kind."

"How so?" I was about to lose it now. Cheating is cheating no matter how much you sugarcoat it.

"A man can have numerous girlfriends, but all his life he will love only one woman, even if she is not the one he married. The reasons why a man cheats are very different from the ones of a woman. When a woman cheats, she does it with her heart and because she never truly loved you and never will."

I left him with his nostalgic and philosophic thoughts, thinking it was too late for him to be saying those "nice things." My phone beeped and it was a text message from Ben:

"Every time I cheat on you, my wife, I understand and learn three truthful things, some old and some new. She has something that you don't and you have something that she doesn't. And me, on the other hand, oh me, I have everything and something that I can never fulfill, something that I always miss..."

This was from a poem I read to him a long time ago.

Why did you go, Ben? Why did you leave me alone? Why couldn't you wait just a little more? I came back as you predicted but you're not there to catch me when I fall on the ground...

Chapter 29

Months were passing by one by one—a bit fast, almost like they were overlapping each other. It was hard to believe Ben was gone, but we started to get used to his absence. Not having him around made me think how many things were taken care of without my realizing it, but Ben would say the same thing about me if I was gone. I put in a new alarm system and better cameras. The system was connected to my phone so I felt much safer that way, thanks to the advanced technology. I couldn't say I felt good or I was okay because nights were difficult and very lonely.

Kris was my best friend and we became very close during that time. I could ask him for anything and he would be there. Sometimes he didn't even need a reason to, and we'd all eat together: me, Ina, him, and his psychologist friend. Sometimes I cooked and sometimes we ordered out, taking turns accordingly with our availability of time. They would order Thai food, or Chinese, and they'd win if we counted votes because they were all fans of it.

I liked certain things as well but that wouldn't be my first choice. I had the privilege of choosing the dessert and he'd always bring some old good wines. Kris had a very sophisticated taste. He belonged to the group of people who say they only have first world problems. Lucky for him, he hadn't had to face any kind of suffering in life. His only worries were how someone overdid it with the spicy sauce, or stuff like that. I teased him here and there about it, but he didn't mind and said that he liked his "problems" and he wished them on everyone.

When you first met him, you might get the impression that he is superficial and the world revolves around him—not true though. Once you got to know him better, you saw how empathic and humanitarian he is. He was very practical in general, even with his feelings. We became so close and best buddies, which allowed us to open up about our worries. Many months had passed since I broke up with Toni, but Kris told me that when I talk about him, I change, and so does my voice, my eyes. He thought the way I explained things about Toni was way too passionate for someone who hurt me deeply. And he said that stories about him were so vivid instead of fading away.

I had a feeling that he thought I wasn't over Toni, regardless of my claiming it was done and that chapter closed. It kind of bothered him that I'd come to Toni's defense sometimes and take the blame for certain things. It bothered him that I talked about Toni like everything had happened just yesterday, but did Kris know that love has just present tense? It never really changes. Kris was trying to convince me that the love I had experienced with Toni might be like those you read in books and see in the movies, the ones that tear your heart apart, but he didn't want to try any one of those.

"I have zero pain tolerance of any kind," he said, smiling ear to ear. He had never been crazy in love with someone in his life. It simply hadn't happened yet, but he had left his heart open and believed that the right person would find the entrance to it someday. The love I had for Toni he called it out of this world, pure and sacred. As for Toni, he thought he was so stupid to lose and let go of that kind of love.

"The problem nowadays," he'd say, "is to find a real, wonderful woman like you, because they all have vaginas, of course."

According to him, love should not be complicated and should be far less painful.

"There are men in your life and loves of your life which sometimes are not the same people. Loves of your life can make you lose your mind and go crazy over them; men in your life will make life a great adventure filled with beautiful things. Loves of your life can make you lose control and not know which direction to go; men in your life will make you feel secure on the ground you step on, and the planet itself, to feel lucky to have you as part of it."

I laughed at his philosophic statements and said that I didn't know doctors could be that deep. "Are you sure you haven't read this somewhere?"

"You're right," he replied with his big smile. "I'm a dentist, not a doctor, by the way, and I might have read it somewhere. I feel romantic lately."

Chapter 30

Ben left to never come back again and I was getting used to that by now. I didn't look at the door anymore waiting for him to enter. Toni was out of my life and I had no clue what he was up to, but life goes on after all. The sun comes out again after the storm. My life was going back to normal and I was recovering fairly well from the stress and pain lately. The guilt I felt toward Ben was replaced now with a deep sadness. I was getting the house ready to put it up for sale and had my realtor looking for a smaller one for me. I didn't want to live alone in that big empty house, and I wanted something smaller, and more cheerful for myself and Ina if she decided to come back after college. I decided to keep the other vacation homes for a while. Ina was doing great and enjoying her college life. She had a boyfriend now whom she'd met there. He was a cute Irish guy from Indiana. Every time I saw them so happy together my heart would jump for joy, but on the other hand, I couldn't help thinking that someday she will start her own family, her own life, but hopefully we'd at least live in the same city.

Oh, how much I missed Toni. I should have forgotten about him by now, but I couldn't, and I didn't know why. Ah, if he had waited a little bit longer. How was he? Was he happy? Had he totally forgotten about me? As for myself, I made peace with the fact that

I could never forget him. He was going to hide secretly in my heart forever. Time after time he'd come into my dreams and I'd feel the burn in my soul from missing him so much. I hadn't seen him in such a long time. Sometimes I had déjà vu moments and sometimes I wished I'd kept the friendship with him at least. One time during one of those special moments of ours, with our bodies wrapped around each other, talking about our future, I brought up the breakup subject. I remember how Toni refused to talk about it. He said, "I don't want to discuss something that I don't want to happen and it won't."

"But," I continued, "just imagine if we broke up, do you know what I'd want? To move as far away from you as possible. I wouldn't want to see you again, or to know where you are and who you are with. Nothing. Everything would finish with you."

"Really, you want that?" Toni asked, surprised. "I would always want to know everything about you even if you'd never want to talk to me again. I would want to know where you live, how you look, if you're happy, and who you're with. I would want to know everything about you, even from a distance. I will live close to you always. I would never want to lose you completely. But none of this will happen because you're not going anywhere and you're mine forever."

"Ah, my luck. Where are you, Toni? I still love you. Nothing can change how I feel about you." Toni couldn't hear me. We had lost the telepathic connection we once had where we would write or call each other at the same time.

Kris had purchased quite a luxurious, beautiful home not too far from me. It was stylish and elegant with big skylights and high ceilings. It was surrounded by a lot of trees and had a breathtaking garden with all kinds of flowers. Further in the back was a pond with plenty of fish. Also it had a huge patio for entertaining with a projector for movies and surround sound, which could be watched from a super nice Jacuzzi that could fit eight people at time. He truly had good taste. He asked me to help with picking out the furniture.

The interior designer gave him all the ideas and projects, but he wanted something more personal that suited him. Who better to contribute to that than people who knew him closely? I did it with pleasure and had a good time doing it. He wasn't close with his psychologist girlfriend anymore, and I wasn't sure if they were really talking. She wasn't his girlfriend, but I thought she might have been one of those "friends with benefits" as they call them now. I didn't ask him any questions after he mentioned once that some relationships expire and can't go any further.

He had a little housewarming party and he invited us all, including Ina's boyfriend, and some of his close friends. When everyone left after the party was over, we stayed to help a little with the cleaning and putting things away. When we were finished and about to leave, he took a glass and hit it lightly with a spoon to get our attention. Then he said that he had a surprise for us. During our conversations, I had talked more than once about how much I loved the Greek islands. As a bonus, his company had given him two tickets to Santorini. Kris was holding the envelope and saying how much we meant to him, how we had been like a family to him and helped him so much.

He considered us some of the closest and most important people in his life, then he pulled out three tickets. With Ina's approval, he had added one more ticket, which he had kept secret to surprise me at that moment.

"What do you think, Ema? This trip is scheduled for August 20."

"Oh no. It is totally unnecessary, Kris. This is too much."

"No need to resist, my friend. Tickets are nonrefundable, so it's done and over, you just have to pack."

I gave in and thanked Kris for his generosity and kindness. I felt a bit sorry for Ina's boyfriend, who was aware of the surprise and had participated but couldn't come with us. He had to work that summer to cover some of his college expenses. Traveling does something to me and I was getting excited. It was only a month away…

Chapter 31

My soul has always marched to the beat of its own drum. The rules that I follow quietly weren't the ones that everyone follows. They were based on my intuition. I follow whatever gives a spark to my emotions. If something sparks my passion, I might sail in troubled waters all my life until my soul finds it. I liked being independent. I was married to a rich man but I have worked to build a successful career myself. I never liked the term "trophy wife," and I could never imagine being one of them myself. I lived in a paradox and didn't know if that was a blessing or a curse. My emotions were extreme. One moment I could be extremely happy and lovely to everyone, another time platonic and completely unplugged from my surroundings. I was unpredictable and nothing in between. I always looked for something new and exciting in life. I hated monotony and that's why I wanted to meet new people and visit faraway places. Sometimes I painted for days and days in a row. Sometimes I crocheted a blanket in two days. Most of all, I'd find pleasure in the little usual things, like a walk to the beach or deep into the woods. I feared love. I feared giving my whole heart to someone because that was all I had. I had loved someone so deeply and unconditionally but I could never trust him fully. Maybe it was because I was afraid to lose my freedom. I kind of knew that I was different. I couldn't change myself but I tried to adjust and be the woman considered "good" by society's standards. Since it was impossible for me to change, I learned how to keep my soul hidden. I was guided by things that feed my soul, like the arts, even though I'm not an artist myself. The right words, the rhythm, and moves are the things that set my soul on fire. I always had this feeling like I have either been in places I visited before or that I should live somewhere else. I believed I had lived different lives in different times. Also, besides my everyday life, I had my fantasy life in my mind, the one filled with passion and adventures as my soul wanted them.

I constantly had a strong desire to live somewhere else. I had no problem packing my luggage and starting a new life somewhere in Australia or Marbella, Spain. I was convinced that I created chaos in my life because, otherwise, I had all the conditions to live a very common and peaceful life. But I find beauty in the imperfections and order out of the mess. That's why it was kind of hard to hold in my emotions. Life was crazy and hard sometimes and so was my heart. For those truthful reasons, it was so hard to cover up what I was going through. It is very hard to put a mask on and pretend things are not difficult when they really are. I also believed in the fantasy of miracles. I believed in the magical happy endings like those in love stories. I believed that the universe had saved some magical things for me to happen in the future and that kept the fire in my soul going...

I was thinking all of this while listening to some good oldies song to break my heart some more. I was listening to Solomon Burke's "Cry to Me" while flying to Santorini...

When we first arrived, our first impression was "this is Santorini?" The airport was small and not very organized. Everyone seemed chilled and slow-paced, unlike us, used to a different rhythm. In America, things were fast-paced and precise. No minute went to waste. That's where the expression "time is money" must have come from. It was really hot and everything started to seem better the moment we saw part of the panoramic view of the beautiful island from the taxi's window. The white houses built in the crater of a volcano from the top down to the deep blue of the Aegean Sea made it so interesting. The sun felt so warm and the sea was as blue as the sky. On every road, wide or narrow, you'd see olive trees full of olives. It was still tourist season and you'd hear all kinds of languages there while cutting through crowds of people.

Everyone was enjoying something in his own way. Some were eating delicious ice cream and some were licking their fingers from juicy pitas and gyros. Others were buying hundreds of souvenirs while some couldn't get enough pictures and selfies taken. I had seen the most beautiful, perfect sunset ever there and that made me feel emotional and all teared up. When the night fell, it was like a dark blanket with shining stars; it was as beautiful but a different atmosphere. It was almost like a theatrical show when they close the curtain to change the scenery for the next part of the show to start. On one side were the white houses with shining lights along the crater and then the dark, black sea crashing light waves against it. The sea was calm and there were many yachts anchored there. If you stood on the balcony to listen to the sounds and feel the vibration of the island, you'd hear characteristic Greek music coming from faraway tavernas and bouzoukis. We had one in our hotel as well. At night tourists dressed in their going-out outfits drank and danced "Zorba's" 'until dawn. In the morning, when everyone was eating breakfast without talking much, they all acted normal, like all the craziness and wildness were gone with the night.

At that time I was getting bursts of unknown happiness and, one time, a burst of sadness that somehow couldn't leave me alone for long. I was getting used to that feeling by now. I always missed something or someone and I had a hole in my chest I couldn't fill. The receptionist offered us a taxi at our disposal to explore the town and it was part of the package. That ended up being one of the best things, for the fact that we didn't have to stress finding places to visit, and usually the islanders know places the tourists don't. His radio was playing Albanian songs and it's amazing how you immediately connect with people you have things in common with. The ice gets broken and you go straight to the questions: Where do you live and what are you up to? Coincidentally, he was from the same city as Toni. When he mentioned the city of his birth, I got chills.

"Eh," I said to myself, "the universe makes it impossible for me to forget Toni. It almost wants me to not forget him, and I don't know why."

Not only that, but once my memories were triggered by a stupid city name, I felt like I saw Toni a couple of times around the island. One time I thought I saw him with a bag coming out of a bakery and getting into a typical rental car, and one time I thought we crossed paths in oncoming traffic. We turned our heads at the same time thinking, how? What? But by the time we turned to get a better look, we had disappeared from each other's eyesight. Ah, that crap that burns my soul from missing him and my mind that was playing those cruel tricks on me. It was a mirage here and there on the stone streets of Santorini, just enough to ruin my peace...

There were only two days left in our vacation and Kris and I were sitting at the bar of the hotel quietly sipping a drink. Through the large windows, I could see how Ina was resting on a chair by the swimming pool and taking in all the warm sun. She had gotten such a nice tan, I thought. Instinctively, as we usually do in places when a TV is on, I was watching the news without really paying any attention. My eyes were there but my mind wasn't. The bartender, who I must say could fix some of the nicest drinks, was talking to Kris and a few other people who were pleasantly enjoying that conversation. Kris would crack a joke and people would laugh and get friendlier with him. I admired his good nature. I was more reserved and was of in my own world for the most part. I needed some time before I warmed up to strangers. But my attention was in all directions.

The TV reporter announced that there was a fatal accident last night and that the couple involved was from the U.S. He went on to identify the two victims. Now the news caught the attention of all the tourists around, who let out a collective "ohh no." The girl was a Green Card from America and the boy was Albanian who was believed to live in the U.S. based on his American driver's license and the Albanian passport found on the scene. The girl was in critical condition fighting for her life, and the boy was pronounced dead at the scene of the crash. The TV reporter was pronouncing their names wrong while their pictures were being shown on the screen.

All of a sudden, my world started to spin uncontrollably and I couldn't keep my equilibrium. I was about to fall on the floor but no one noticed that I wasn't okay. I couldn't say a sound to let them know either. The bartender was into her conversation and said sadly, "Oh, they got the curse of the island. People not only don't know, but when they do, they don't realize how true and dangerous it is."

This sparked Kris's interest and he wanted to know what exactly what she meant by "curse of the island."

"Santorini," she explained passionately, "is not a place to be visited with someone you just met, or someone who you are not truly in love with. You are supposed to be here only with someone you love deeply, otherwise you get cursed and your relationship will get ruined. It is a fact that many couples announce breakups after visiting Santorini, or worse; one, and sometimes both, never leave the island. For such a little island with not many cars or people, the number of fatal car accidents is outrageous. Freaky accidents happen here and not just with cars—sometimes walking, or climbing the hills."

Kris, who was now mesmerized by that legend, turned around to see if I was listening, but jumped when he saw my face was as white as paper.

"Ema, are you okay?"

"Is there something wrong with your wife?" the bartender asked.

"Oh, she is not my wife. Do you want me to take you to your room? You're so pale."

I didn't talk, just nodded my approval and walked, holding his arm and letting hot tears fall from my cheeks to my chest.

"Is it him?!" Kris asked, terrified.

I nodded again because no words would come out of my mouth. I burst out crying, louder now, and crashed into my bed with my face hidden in the pillow. I gave Kris a sign to leave the room. He quietly did without asking, and I let myself scream and cry out all my grief. I was crying not only with tears, but with words as well, directed to someone in the universe. Maybe Toni's spirit was around and I was talking to him.

"Oh, Toni, my love. I don't know why the universe is always bringing us so close and then separating us again. Oh, what a cruel life. Toni, my love, why did you go? You were so young." All the pain was trying to come out of my chest in the most agonizing way, I thought I would stop breathing while I was crying.

"Oh, my love, I could never hate you. You were my pain, my love, my everything. You were the only one I ever loved, the only true, real thing. I forgive you, my love. We will meet each other again in a different life, like we used to tell each other. Rest in peace, Toni. I love you forever..."

www.ingramcontent.com/pod-product-compliance
Lightning Source LLC
Chambersburg PA
CBHW070525100726
47907CB00004B/991